THE MUSTANG MACHINE

The Mustang Machine is the best bike in the universe, according to Mr Amos. It's a wild bike, an untamed bike, and whoever can catch and brand it will be its master.

Not only that, but if it's tamed by Tim's gang, they'll be sure to win the bike-riding contest at the Spring Fayre, which won't please Dennis Doggerty, the local bully.

D0957746

OTHER BOOKS BY CHRIS POWLING

Roald Dahl
Puffin

The Conker as Hard as a Diamond
Puffin

Gorgeous George
Orchard

Hiccup Harry
Collins

The Phantom Carwash
Egmont

Long John Santa
Macdonald

My Sister's Name is Rover
A & C Black

A Book about Books
A & C Black

CHRIS POWLING *The*
Mustang
Machine

BARN OWL BOOKS

First published in Great Britain 1981
by Abelard-Schuman Limited
This edition first published 2000 by Barn Owl Books
15 New Cavendish Street, London W1M 7RL
Barn Owl Books are distributed by
Frances Lincoln

Text copyright © 1981, 2000 Chris Powling
The moral right of Chris Powling to be identified as
author of this work has been asserted

ISBN 1 903015 06 5
A CIP catalogue record for this book
is available from the British Library

Designed and typeset by
Douglas Martin Associates
Printed and bound in Great Britain by
Cox & Wyman Limited, Reading

For Pat Powling

FIRST INVENTOR OF THE MUSTANG MACHINE

¶ One

Old, scruffy Mr Amos first told Becca about the Mustang Machine. The best bike in the universe, he called it.

"Is there such a thing?" she asked. "Truly?"

"You bet there is."

Becca sighed.

"I'd settle for the worst bike in the universe. I'd settle for any bike at all. So would Tim or Sharon or the twins. At least then one of our gang could *enter* the Contest even if we didn't win it."

"Which Contest would that be?" said Mr Amos.

She knew he was teasing but she told him anyway.

"The bike-riding Contest at the Spring Fayre. It's for twelve-year-olds and under. Last year was the first ever – and that rotten bully Dennis Doggerty was the winner. He'll win again this year, probably. He's been practising for months. So has every other kid we know. Even if we did get hold of the best bike in the universe it's too late to catch up now."

"Don't you believe it, young lady. With the Mustang Machine anything is possible. Strikes me you don't know very much about the Mustang Machine."

"First I've heard of it," admitted Becca.

"Really? You mean I've never mentioned it before?"

"Never. Tell me now, Mr Amos – please."

"Certainly I will. Just give me a second to get me thoughts tidy."

Becca sat back and patiently. Mr Amos's stories were always worth waiting for. Eventually, after he'd banged his pipe against the fire-grate and made his spectacles even dirtier by rubbing them on the sleeve of his cardigan, he began.

"Properly speaking, I only saw the Mustang Machine once," he said. "Just the once, Becca. About your age, I was, and I was only knee high to a grasshopper just like you. Yet I remember it as clearly as if it were only a couple of ticks ago . . .

"Yes, only a couple of ticks ago . . . nigh on seventy years. I was on my way to the corner-shop, I remember, to get some pie-and-mash for our supper. It was dark and icy and so quiet if you stood still and listened hard enough you could have heard your own heartbeat. I was thinking about rich kids, Becca – rich kids who owned bikes. I was jealous, you see, because I'd have given anything in the world to have a bike of my own. To tell you the truth, I wanted one so much I hated the sound of my own boots going clump-clump-clump on the pavement. What I really longed to hear was swish-and-click, swish-and-click, swish-and-click – the sound of a bike. My bike. With me on it.

"The trouble was, in those days only rich kids had bikes and I wasn't a rich kid. So that was that. I was stuck with getting to that corner-shop on foot – and getting home fast before Jack Frost got his chilly mitts round our pie-and-mash, otherwise I'd get a clip round the ear. Very particular about having his pie-and-mash *hot* my Dad was.

"Then I heard it, Becca: swish-and-click, swish-and-click, swish-and-click . . . a luxury bike if ever I heard one!

"But where was it? The street was deserted and so were all the side-turnings. Yet it seemed so close: swish-and-click, swish-and-click, swish-and-click. Almost on top of me – that's the way it sounded. And that's what made me look up. Up to the roof-tops.

"And, Golly Moses, there the bike was. It was gliding over the roof-tops neat as blow-me-a-kiss. Up and down and

8

around it went and there wasn't a chimney or a gutter or a dormer window could stop it: swish-and-click, swish-and-click, swish-and-click. Ah, right grand it looked, glinting up there in the moonlight. Never since bikes were first thought of has there been a bike like that one, Becca. It was so magnificent I wasn't surprised at all that it didn't travel along the ground like as if it were *ordinary*.

"Something else didn't surprise me, either. The saddle was empty. Yes, empty. *There was no rider*. Now that could mean only one thing. It was a wild bike, an untamed bike, a maverick bike. And whoever could catch it and break it in would be its master. But that wouldn't be easy. Even as I gazed at it, the bike vanished – but not before it had reared right up on its back wheel for all the world like a prancing stallion: the Mustang Machine.

"I don't mind telling you the pie-and-mash was stone-cold by the time I got home that night and I got my ear clipped good and proper. But after that I never stopped looking for the Mustang Machine. Once or twice it did seem to me I caught a glimpse of it, too – a sudden glitter of spokes along some telegraph-wires, a flash of handlebars in a tree-top. Oh yes . . . I never stopped looking and I never stopped hoping. Not for seventy years."

Mr Amos sucked at his pipe and stared into the fire.

"Didn't you ever get a bike of your own?" Becca asked.

"Not when I was a kid, I didn't. Remember, only rich kids got bikes in those days."

"But if you'd captured it, and tamed it, would the Mustang Machine really have belonged to you?"

"Certainly it would. Stands to reason, doesn't it? Naturally, you'd have to brand it."

"*Brand* it?"

"Make your mark on it. So everyone could tell straightaway it was yours. Not that anyone could ever steal it, Becca.

Gracious me, no. Only one person can ride the Mustang Machine and that's its rightful owner. Anyone else would get bunged up in the air so high it would be Tuesday fortnight before they hit the ground. That's why you'd need to brand it, you see. To warn people off."

"And would the rightful owner be able to ride it up there on the rooftops?"

"Roof-tops, tree-tops, mountain-tops. They're all the same to the Mustang Machine. Wouldn't surprise me if the Mustang Machine couldn't manage a half-dozen rainbows, a couple of thunderclouds and a quick shufty round the solar system all before breakfast!"

After this Mr Amos laughed so much he started to choke and Becca had to thump his back till he stopped coughing.

"You were joking," she wailed. "You were pulling my leg the whole time!"

"Who me?" said Mr Amos.

And he laughed all over again which led to more choking and more thumps.

"Thank you, my dear, thank you," he said afterwards. "Now you'd better be on your way or I'll have your mum after me. When shall I see you again?"

"Soon," promised Becca. "And thank you again for the story, Mr Amos."

"Like it, did you?"

"It was smashing."

"I'm glad. There's nothing like a good story, I always say."

"Nothing," sighed Becca.

For that was the trouble. Nothing was ever like a good story. You don't come across the Mustang Machine in real life even if Mr Amos did get you believing in it for a minute or two. In real life it was always kids like Dennis Doggerty who won the Contest. Still, she'd enjoy telling Sharon and Georgie and Leroy and Tim about the best bike in the universe. Even if it wasn't true it made you feel better.

On the doorstep Becca turned back to Mr Amos.

"What story will you tell me next?" she asked.

There was no answer.

"Mr Amos?"

Still he said nothing. The old man was staring up at the telegraph wires along the street with a faraway look in his eyes that seemed to stretch back seventy years and a couple of ticks. Becca gasped – then realised he was fooling her all over again.

"Stop it!" she giggled. "The Mustang Machine! What a spoofer you are!"

"Who me?" said Mr Amos.

¶ Two

Becca knew just the place to tell the gang about the Mustang Machine. It was called the Point – a name she had never understood since it was as flat and bare as a football pitch. All round it, the Point had bushes, trees and a spiky railing to stop kids hurtling over the brink and crash-landing in the backyards below. For the Point was at the top of a hill and the rest of the city seemed to fall away from it. First you saw the winding huddle of terraces where Becca and her mates lived, then lower down came the smart, white crescents of the posh houses and after that began a muddle that lasted as far as the horizon – factories and high-rise flats and the river with its cranes and wharfs, all mirrored on the other side by more flats and factories and houses and terraces and maybe even other hills called the Point, for all Becca knew.

"A wild bike?" exclaimed Georgie, when she'd finished.

"That's what he said."

"And if you captured it you could keep it?"

Becca nodded.

"And only you could ride it because it's a sort of bucking-bronco bike that rides up walls and along parapets and anywhere you want to go?"

"Yes."

"Sounds more like a sort of witch's-broom bike," said Sharon. "You know, one that can only be ridden at the dead of night."

"Mr Amos didn't say that. I think it just happened to be night-time when he saw it."

12

"And I bet it just happened to be closing-time at the pub, too," Leroy scoffed. "I bet he was boozed."

"Why don't you get those big ears cleaned out," said Georgie. "He was only a kid when he saw it. She told you that. Seventy years ago it happened – isn't that right, Becca?"

"When he was our age."

"There you are then," said Sharon. "That's the olden days. There was magic about in the olden days."

"Magic!" snorted Leroy. "It's just a story I tell you. He's always telling her stories. If you'd been listening you'd have heard that, too."

"I . . . don't know," said Tim.

Straightaway they were quiet. They always listened to Tim. Even Georgie and Leroy stopped bickering when Tim spoke. They both stared at him now – their twin pairs of eyes and twin sets of teeth gleaming from twin black faces that were so much alike it was hard to believe one wasn't a reflection of the other . . . though which was which? Georgie – Leroy or Leroy – Georgie? Even Sharon couldn't tell them apart and she was their sister.

Tim kept them waiting. He didn't do this to show he was the leader. Tim wasn't like that. It was because he hadn't made up his mind what he wanted to say and these days Tim never wasted a word just as he never wasted a movement and never wasted a breath. He couldn't afford to, what with his thinness and the dim red flush in his cheeks. No one was quite sure what was wrong with Tim but it was whispered that the next time he went into hospital he'd never come out.

"That Mr Amos," he said eventually. "He's lived round here all his life, hasn't he?"

"That's right," said Sharon. "In the self-same house."

"So it must've been round here he saw the Mustang Machine . . ."

13

"See what I mean?" Leroy interrupted. "Kindly tell me where there's a corner-shop selling pie-and-mash round here!"

"Not now, you dimbo," snorted Georgie. "There aren't pie-and-mash shops *anywhere* now. But there were plenty of them years ago. Kindly tell me how I got lumbered with a dimbo twin-brother like you."

"Kindly tell me how I got lumbered with *two* dimbo twin brothers," said Sharon. "Just listen to Tim, can't you?"

Tim was still pondering. Becca stared at him, puzzled. What was he getting at?

"And it looks *special*, somehow . . . but the noise it makes is the same as any other bike?"

"Swish-and-click, swish-and-click, swish-and-click," Becca said. "Changing as it gets faster, of course. That's how he described it, Tim."

"I see."

What did Tim see? As usual, his eyes were bright from his illness – 'hectic' Becca's Mum called them – but right now they had an extra sparkle that seemed to light up his whole face. Georgie, Leroy, Sharon and Becca glanced at each other uneasily. It was when Tim was like this that they worried about him most.

"I've *seen* it," he announced softly.

"What?"

"Up on the railway embankment. A couple of months ago. It was just getting dark but the street-lamps had come on so I couldn't possibly miss it."

Leroy cleared his throat.

"What . . . er . . . what was it you thought you saw, Tim?" he asked.

"The Mustang Machine," Tim said. "Isn't that what we've been talking about for the last –" he looked at his watch – "nineteen minutes?"

14

"Sure, Tim. But it was probably . . . you know . . . a trick of the light. Everything looks a bit funny when it's dark."

Tim shook his head.

"Not that funny. Not a bike without a rider that kicks up its front wheels as if it's pawing the air, then plunges over the arch of the railway bridge and disappears into the tunnel *upside-down* with its tyres swishing along the underside of the tunnel-roof. I could even hear dirt and gunge and bits of rubble falling on the track."

"What happened then?" Sharon gasped.

"Nothing. It vanished."

"Vanished?"

"Out of the other side of the tunnel, I suppose. It simply . . . went."

"Just like with Mr Amos," said Becca.

"At first I reckoned I must be going barmy. Maybe it was my new medicine, I thought. That's why I haven't mentioned it before. But now I know what it was: the Mustang Machine."

"Magic," breathed Sharon, "like in the olden days."

This was a shivery thought. Maybe the Mustang Machine would appear right now, bouncing along the spiked tops of the Point's railings, perhaps.

"Anyway," sniffed Leroy, "I prefer real-life bikes. Like those ones over there."

He jerked his thumb. Over the crest of the Point had come a sudden stampede of cycles. The bright sunlight and the blue sky showed them off perfectly and each of the riders knew it. They whooped and yelled as if this were their victory lap after a triumphant two-wheeled tour of the world.

"Big kids," said Becca.

"Rich kids," said Georgie and Leroy. "Just look at their machines."

15

"Just look at their faces," said Sharon grimly. "That's Dennis Doggerty and his gang – the famous Gents."

Georgie whistled.

"She's right. It's Dennis Dogsmuck, in person."

"You'd better not call him that to his face. He'll tear up a tree and brain you with it – assuming he can find your brains."

"Dennis is all mouth," said Leroy.

"Yeah, and his mouth is full of teeth like a shark. They say he's even more of a hard case now he's at secondary school."

"Wouldn't mind a close look at that new bike of his," Georgie said.

"Must be your lucky day then. He's coming over. And don't forget, you two, his name is Doggerty, *not* Dogsmuck."

Sharon broke off hastily. When Dennis and his Gents approached, you watched what you said.

Raising his hand like a cavalry commander halting a troop, Dennis skidded his bike to a stop. His Gents pulled up behind him in a slither of tyres. Gravel spattered and pinged against the railings.

Dennis eased himself back in the saddle. He was called Dogsmuck – by people far enough away – for more reasons than his surname. Whatever clothes he was wearing, there was always something slimily brown about Dennis. Perhaps it was his gingery hair or the colour of his eyes or his skin blotched all over with freckles. Also, it may have been because you avoided both dogsmuck and Dennis whenever you could. Unless you were one of his Gents, of course. Most of the time Dennis was surrounded by his Gents. Here they all were right now: Weasel Bates, Stevie Spinks, Hogan Wade and Madboy Sullivan – plus two or three other toughies the gang had picked up now they were at secondary school.

But Dennis was still the boss. You could tell that at a glance. The Gents' eyes kept flicking back to him, ready to leap into action if he gave an order. They even copied the way he brushed a speck of dust off the paintwork of his bike.

And what a bike!

Becca and Sharon, Georgie, Leroy and Tim stood and gaped, not missing a detail.

"Having a good noss?" grated Dennis. "Taking it all in, are you?"

He was talking to them all but everyone knew it was Tim, their leader, who had to reply.

"Don't see you round here very often, Dennis," he answered carefully. "Not your usual territory, is it?"

Dennis checked the button on one of his riding gloves, flexing his fingers so that one moment his hand made a claw, the next a fist.

"Quite right, Timothy, my old son," he said. "But things have changed. Yes, completely changed, things have. You may have noticed that we are fully mobile, me and my Gents here. We are in a condition, you might say, of total vehicular transport. Which means we can cover *more* territory. In fact, at any given moment nobody can be quite sure *where* we are. It's a case, Timothy, of now you see us, now you don't. And then again, now you don't see us . . . and now, all of a naffin' sudden, you *do*. Get my meaning?"

Tim nodded.

"I can just about work it out."

"You can?"

"Yes."

"Handsome," declared Dennis. "For a primary school kid I call that a handsome piece of working out. What do you reckon, Gents?"

"Handsome, Dennis!" they chorused.

"So watch your step, my darlin' little Timothy. You might just be treading on my territory. Okay? I said – *okay*?"

"Okay."

"Handsome. Utterly handsome. Did you hear that, Gents? Message received and message understood."

Dennis lifted his glove in a wagons-ho gesture. But before anyone could move, Madboy Sullivan spoke.

"Is that all, Dennis? Aren't we going to duff them up a bit?"

Dennis considered the idea.

"No, Madboy," he said. "Not on this occasion. We've just cleaned the bikes, haven't we? Suppose some of their blood got splashed on our beautiful bodywork? Can't have that. Besides, just look at them. Are they worth duffin' up? Look at her, for example . . ."

His muddy eyes slid over Becca from her hair-ribbon to her patent-leather shoes.

"Just a Mummy's little sweety-pie, she is. And look at them . . ." He shifted his gaze to Sharon, Georgie and Leroy. "Who are they, may I ask? Just three naffin' little wogs . . ."

"Take no notice," Tim hissed.

He needn't have worried. Sharon, Georgie and Leroy were stony-faced.

"And as for him," Dennis went on, "old puff-and-blow Timothy over there, well word has it he's busy duffin' himself up. From the inside outwards. Have you coughed up anything interesting lately, Timothy, my old son? Anything, as you might say, *vital*? You know, if you're not careful, your *coughing* is going to lead to your *coffin* . . ."

"Shut your face!" came a girl's voice.

"Eh?" Dennis said.

"Just shut your face!" Becca screeched again.

"You talking to me, kid?"

"Yes, I'm talking to you – to *you*! To stinky, slimy Dogs-muck Doggerty!"

Even Dennis himself gasped. But Becca hadn't finished yet.

"And this is what I think of your dogs-bum bicycle!"

Savagely she kicked out. There was a clang like strings snapping in a small, steel harp. No one moved. Slowly, tremblingly, Becca pulled her foot from the spokes and backed away. Dennis's voice, when it came, was all the more chilling for being dazed with shock.

"She's smashed it," he whispered. "She's smashed my naffin' machine . . ."

Yet it was Tim's voice that was really terrifying. Never before had they heard him so snappy.

"Run, Becca! Don't just stand there – run!"

¶ Three

There was only one way Becca could escape. She reached the railings just ahead of Sharon.

"Quick –give me a lift up!"

"She's getting away!" Dennis snarled. "Stop her!"

Becca was already straddling the spikes. She swung her legs, hung for a moment at arm's length, then let go. To her relief the foot of the embankment came sooner than she expected, and softer: a mound of grass years high.

"Look out, Becca!"

Down came Sharon too, half-falling, half-slithering.

"Thought you'd need some help," she explained, spitting out grass.

"Thanks," said Becca, "but which way do we go?"

Back-gardens stretched away on either side of them, fence after fence.

"Can't climb over those," said Sharon. "By the time we got clear they'd be waiting for us. Last I saw of them they were already trying to head us off."

"What about Tim? And Leroy and Georgie?"

Sharon grinned.

"Don't worry, Becca. It's *you* Dennis wants. And if we don't move fast, he's going to get you, too."

"So which way?"

"This way."

As if she owned the place, Sharon marched down the garden. Loudly she banged on the back door.

"You can't do that," Becca protested.

"I'm doing it."

Sharon knocked again, even louder.

"Who's that?" came a voice.

They heard footsteps, then the rattle of a bolt. It was a large, fat man who opened the door. He pushed back his cap in surprise.

"Who are you?" he demanded.

"We got lost," said Sharon. "Thanks for helping us, mister."

Grabbing Becca's hand, she pushed past him into the dark, dank hallway.

"Front-door this way, mister? Oh yes, there it is."

"Just you hold on a minute. How come you got lost in my backyard? Nobody can get *into* my backyard."

"Bye, mister," called Sharon.

Outside, the street was empty. They were well ahead of Dennis . . . so far.

"Quick, Becca. Over there – the alleyway. It's too steep for bikes."

"They're coming, Sharon! I'm sure I can hear them."

"So don't waste your breath – get moving!"

The alleyway was almost too steep for pedestrians, never mind bikes. Like a staircase of paving-slabs it zigzagged down the hill. They took two steps at a time, their feet echoing so loudly it seemed to Becca all Dennis had to do was pinpoint the sound and set up an ambush. Had Sharon realised this?

"Down here!"

Sharon swung left, off the main alley, into a passage that was no more than a rough track. Even in May it looked overgrown.

"Stop behind that tree. We need a plan, Becca."

Of course Sharon had realised – Scaredycat Sharon, a believer in ghosts and vampires and wizards but with a brain as fast as Tim's in an emergency. Even as she got her breath back she was thinking aloud.

"A plan . . . now, let me see. Does Dennis know where you live?"

"Shouldn't think so. He comes from the other side of the railway-line, doesn't he?"

"Miles away," said Sharon. "Well, getting on for a mile anyway. So he can't have your house staked out?"

"No, but he and his mates could just be cruising around, waiting. He knows we can't dodge around these alleyways for ever. Sooner or later we've got to come out on a street."

"Right. But he doesn't know which street. That gives us a chance, Becca. Especially with a decoy . . ."

"A decoy? What decoy?"

"Me."

"You mean . . . ?"

"We change clothes – then you lie low for an hour while I lead Dennis and his Gents away from here. By then it'll be dusk. Much easier for you to get home."

"But suppose he catches you, Sharon?"

"Suppose he does? It's not me he's after is it? I'll just blub and beg for mercy. Anyway, have you got a better idea? Course you haven't. So let's give mine a try. We're both wearing jeans so all we've got to do is swap your duffle-coat for my parka."

"Good job we're the same size."

"Right. Better pull our hoods up, though. Even Dennis can tell the difference between black and white."

"Okay. And . . . Sharon?"

"Yes?"

"Thanks."

"Forget it. I feel like a bit of exercise. Don't try for home till it gets dark. See you, Becca."

"See you."

At the main alleyway Sharon turned to wave, then vanished.

22

Uneasily, Becca looked round her. Now she was alone, everything seemed to shift and twitch so much more. Even the rattle of the wind in the wire fence sounded louder. She shivered. If only she were brave like Sharon. Sharon might cross her fingers, touch wood, never walk under ladders and avoid every crack in the pavement, yet she was always brave. Take now, for example. While Sharon was off tricking Dennis and his Gents, all Becca wanted to do was find somewhere to hide, somewhere warm preferably. She sniffed. Was that a bonfire smell?

As Becca followed the track there was soon smoke, too. Bluer and thicker with every step, it led her round a curve and though an arch of thin, spindly trees. These screened a stableyard and here was the fire – banked up in front of a row of horse-boxes so dilapidated one loud whinny would have collapsed them all.

"Is anybody here?" Becca called.

In this sad place which seemed so faraway and forgotten despite being hemmed in on every side? At one end the stable roof had slipped to ground level, spilling bricks and slates over the cobblestones. Every surface was splashed with bird lime. The sour stink of cats hung in the air. Becca wrinkled her nose. What a dump!

Except, that is, at the upright end of the stable. Here was a clean, weatherproof cranny the size of a bus shelter. Someone was keeping it tidy. The same person who'd lit the bonfire?

"Do you mind if I wait here?" Becca called again. "Whoever you are?"

No answer. She settled herself in a crook of woodwork and stone which was all that was left of a horse's manger. At last she was cosy – with a view of the track that gave her a fifty-yard start on anyone who approached. Not a bad den, really.

Becca yawned. How much time had already passed? Surely the sky was less bright? And wasn't it much, much colder? Thank goodness for the fire.

Another yawn.

Did you always feel sleepy when you were scared? She bet Sharon didn't. Or Georgie, or Leroy. But if she were sick like Tim she'd be sleepy all the time . . .

Becca wasn't sure what woke her up. Perhaps it was cramp or the sharp chill now that the fire had burned down. Whatever it was she was grateful because something else was stirring out there in the twilight. The sound made her gasp.

"It can't be," she said.

She listened again It was just as Mr Amos had described in his story.

"It . . . it just can't be," she whispered.

But it was. And it was coming closer.

Swish-and-click, swish-and-click, swish-and-click.

¶ Four

Up and up the zigzagging steps.

At the top would be the Doggerty gang. They'd soon spot the dufflecoat. Then the chase would start. She'd dodge back into the alleyways, luring them after her. Away from their bikes they'd have no chance, for who could run faster than Sharon? Under fences, through barbed-wire, along the tops of walls, she'd lead them further and further from Becca till she had them doubled up from the stitch in their sides.

Unless they separated, that is, and headed her off. What would happen then?

Sharon knew what would happen then. When Dennis was still at primary school, she'd seen what he did to kids who challenged him. At the very least it would be the Jungle Treatment. Sharon shuddered and slowed down. The Jungle Treatment . . .

First would come spiky-spiders. Stevie Spinks was the expert at spiky-spiders. They'd push her flat on her back, then Stevie would hover over her with crooked, twitching fingers. At first his nails would brush on her skin no worse than tickling, but gradually the tickle would seem to grow talons as he pinch-pinch-pinched. Tomorrow she'd still be able to see the marks Stevie left on her.

Next, it would be the elephant-walk. The elephant-walk was Hogan Wade's speciality. With his knees pinning down her arms, he'd sit on her stomach and pound her chest with his fists – clump-clump-clump – till every one of her ribs felt bruised. Even then the torture wasn't over.

"Stop blubbing," Dennis would sneer. "You've still got python-the-ponk to come."

"No! Please," she'd beg, "not python-the-ponk."

"Sorry, kid. Python-the-ponk coming up. How can you have the Jungle Treatment without python-the-ponk? Ready Madboy?"

Madboy Sullivan had practised python-the-ponk for hours. No one could do it better. Sharon sometimes had nightmares about it. What she really hated wasn't the thought of Madboy's arms slithering over her, it was his hands snapping open-and-shut in a snake-like way as he dropped dirt up her sleeve and down her neck and into her nose and ears. When it came to the slither-and-snap of python-the-ponk you had to shut your mouth tight however hard you'd been screaming up till then. Did Madboy keep that filthy pair of gloves especially for python-the-ponk?

But the worst part of the Jungle Treatment would be Dennis. Always, Dennis saved himself till last.

"You look miserable, kid," he'd say. "All hot and bothered are you? Now don't worry, we'll soon put that right. Okay, Gents? Tarzan's waterfall?"

"Tarzan's waterfall it is, Dennis," they'd snigger.

The Jungle Treatment always finished with Tarzan's waterfall however much fuss you kicked up. You could shout, you could plead, you could offer your pocket money for the rest of your life but Dennis would never let you off. Still, you'd be dragged to the nearest toilet and made to kneel down. Inch by inch your head would be forced into the lavatory-bowl. Just when you thought your neck was about to snap and you couldn't hold your breath any longer, Dennis would pull the chain.

Sharon squirmed. Was she really prepared to risk all that just for Becca? Did she really *like* Becca? When she thought

26

of Becca's posh way of talking and of the airs and graces Becca's mum gave herself even though everyone in the street knew Becca had never had a dad, not really, and that was why they'd moved there . . . well, Sharon did sometimes wonder why Tim had invited Becca to join the gang in the first place.

"She'll do," was all he'd said.

And to be fair Becca had done all right. True, she was as niminy-piminy as ever but she never backed down on anything even when she was shaking with fright. In fact, Becca was often the bravest of all of them. Look what she'd done to Dennis's bike, for example. *And* she was the only kid who'd ever dared call him 'dogsmuck' to his face. Sharon grinned. Of course she would help Becca.

She'd better make sure of her luck, though. Slowly she crossed her fingers, her arms, her legs and her eyes. Also she crossed her heart and hoped to die but not just yet and not from Dennis. When she'd done all this three times over, she started up the slope again.

Where the alley met the street, she paused. The Gents were bound to be there somewhere. But the further she moved into bike territory, the easier she'd be to catch. So how could she attract their attention? Come on Sharon, think. You're supposed to be the brainy one of the family. *Think*, Sharon.

Sharon cleared her throat, threw back her shoulders and began to sing. The tune was *Happy Birthday* but not the words:

"Dennis Dogsmuck, Boo-Hoo!
Dennis Dogsmuck – what a Poo!
Don't tread in Dennis Dogsmuck,
He's yukky through and through!"

Five times Sharon sang her song. Each repeat grew louder

and sharper till her voice echoed through the streets, shrill as a tomcat trapped in a tunnel. Did she sound like Becca? Would her face be masked enough by the hood of the duffle-coat? Could they hear her anyway?

"Dennis Dogsmuck, Boo Hoo!
Dennis Dogsmuck – what a Poo!"

Yes, they'd heard.

They gathered down at the corner. She saw Madboy Sullivan pointing towards her, giving orders. Weasel Bates and a couple of the new gang members swung their bikes away into a side-street. In a moment they'd reappear at the opposite corner, cutting her off. Then, at a signal from Madboy, they'd advance. Madboy was always in command when Dennis wasn't around.

"Don't tread in Dennis Dogsmuck,
He's yukky through and through!"

And there they were – Weasel Bates plus escort. Madboy lifted his hand in an exact copy of Dennis. Sharon sniffed. What did she care? With the alleyways behind her she was quite safe. Once the Gents were off those bikes they'd lost their advantage. She was the queen of the alleyways, providing she stayed ahead of an ambush. So let Madboy make the most of his turn as Big Boss. He'd be number two again soon enough once Dennis got back from wherever he was.

From wherever he was . . . which wasn't with Madboy, Hogan, Stevie or the others.

Where was Dennis, then?

Sharon felt the first prickle of fear. It ran down her spine like the touch of icy fingers. Even before she looked behind her, she knew exactly where Dennis was.

"Hello," she croaked.

"Time for naffin' choir-practice, is it?" said Dennis.

In a half-crouch, his arms spread, he blocked off the alley.

"Dogsmuck?" he said. "Is that what I am?"

Quickly, Sharon looked right and left. Too late. Already the Gents were on their way. They came without hurry. Why rush when Dennis had everything under control?

"Where is she?"

"You mean – ?"

"You know who I mean. You're wearing her coat."

Sharon swallowed.

"I don't know where she is."

"Now that is a pity. That is a naffin' great pity, that is. 'Cos now I shall have to do to you what I intend to do to her when I catch up with her. And I will catch up with her. Ho, yes. Not today, maybe. Maybe not even tomorrow. But one day very soon she will get caught up with. You can reckon on that. And I will make sure she never forgets it."

"What . . . what are you going to do?"

"Good question. Very good question. What are we going to do, Gents?"

They were all round her now, a half-circle of bikes barricading the kerb and the pavement.

"Python-the-ponk," said Madboy.

"The elephant-walk," Hogan Wade said.

"Spiky-spiders," giggled Stevie Spinks.

"The full Jungle Treatment," Weasel Bates insisted, "with Tarzan's waterfall to finish off."

Dennis's muddy eyes glinted.

"Kid's stuff," he said.

"What?"

"Kid's stuff. This calls for something . . . special."

Sharon felt sick. If the Jungle Treatment was kid's stuff what would the grown-up stuff be like? And why couldn't she shift her eyes from Dennis? Absent-mindedly, he was picking a pimple on his chin with a dirty fingernail. Every so

29

often he sucked off what he picked. He wasn't looking at her. She wasn't important – just a victim. In fact, he wasn't looking at anybody. Dennis went into a sort of trance when he was inventing a new torment.

"Know something?" he said at last. "I'm magic. I ought to get a Nobel prize, I ought. What d'you reckon?"

"Sure Dennis," agreed the Gents.

"Yeah. That's what I deserve – along with a knighthood in the naffin' New Year's Honours List."

"How come, Dennis?" asked Madboy.

"Because I am a genius, my old son Sullivan. No one is more genius-er than I am. Ho, no. Not after what I've just thought up."

Everyone waited. Dennis always smacked his lips a bit before he told you what was on the menu. He was grinning now, showing stained and crooked teeth. Even his tongue looked mossy.

"Madboy," he said, "remember our visit to the Chamber of Horrors?"

"Yes."

"Well, think of the worst thing you saw there. Yes, let's all of us do that . . . sort of conjure up in our minds the foulest exhibit of the whole naffin' lot. Okay?"

"Okay, Dennis."

Sharon had been on that trip. A young teacher had taken them there and by mistake had led them into the display that was for Adults Only. Three kids had wet themselves. Another had fainted. Desperately, Sharon tried to keep out of her thoughts her personal terror – that small, hideous waxwork she'd come across in a side-gallery. For weeks afterwards the memory of it had kept her awake . . .

"No," she whimpered.

"Got a clear picture, have you?" said Dennis. "Every detail sharp?"

"No!"

"No? Keep working at it then. 'Cos I want you in the right mood for what I've got planned for you and for your hoity-toity mate. First it'll be your turn . . . so you can tell her all about it in advance. Something to look forward to, you might say. Then it'll be her turn – probably even better because we'll have had a bit of practice on you. And when I say 'better' I don't actually mean *better*, if you get my meaning."

Sharon got his meaning. Dennis was no ordinary bully. Always he kept in strict training – drenching himself in nastiness the way you soak a conker in vinegar. She could never decide which frightened her the more, Dennis's tortures or Dennis's tongue. He had most kids screaming for mercy before he even touched them. But always, in the end, he touched them.

Sharon sighed. Why put it off then?

"All right," she said. "I'll tell you how to find Becca."

"Good. How?"

"Follow the smell of mothballs."

"What?"

"And fresh-air spray."

"Eh?"

"And disinfectant."

"What are you on about?"

Sharon took a deep breath.

"Well, she came into contact with your bike, didn't she, Dennis? So she's got to get rid of the stink somehow."

There was a moment of silence. Then, behind her, Sharon heard the rustle of legs dismounting from bikes and the soft thud of stands snapping into place. Dennis hadn't said a word. He didn't need to. His Gents knew exactly what they had to do. Cross my heart and hope to die, Sharon thought.

She shut her eyes tight . . . so what happened next came only as a soundtrack.

It began with a sudden clang, followed by more clangs, one after the other just as if a row of bikes had been toppled like dominoes. Also there were yells . . . angry at first, then turning to panic. After this came scuffling as Dennis staggered and fell. By the time Sharon's eyes were wide open he was already flat on his back. This was all the chance she needed. She half-dodged him, half-leapt over him and ran, ran, ran but not because she expected to be chased. No one would chase her now. What she wanted to leave behind was that *other* sound – the sound which had caused all the trouble. Even now it seemed to fill her ears.

Swish-and-click, swish-and-click, swish-and-click.

¶ Five

Back at the Point, Tim, Georgie and Leroy had no idea they were about to witness a Miracle.

"Be nice to Dennis?" Leroy was saying. "Why should we be nice to Dennis? Dennis is never nice to us."

"He wouldn't know how," said Georgie.

Tim shrugged.

"That's what I mean. Maybe he needs to be *shown* how."

"By *us*?"

"Sure, Leroy. Why not? Someone's got to get him started."

"Yeah, someone. Someone who'll get finished off trying to do it. I can see it now. Hello, Dennis. Lovely weather we're having. ZONK! Oh dear, Dennis, my teeth seem to have bumped into your fist. No, don't worry – I'll pick up the bits. Shall I lick your boots while I'm down here? THUMP! Cor, thank you Dennis, I've always wanted a cauliflower-ear. BASH! Two cauliflower-ears, I mean. You're a real prince, Dennis, taking all this trouble. POW! Ah, look at that – blood. My favourite. Especially when it's pouring out of my nose. How did you know I like red best of all, Dennis? SLAM! Except for black, of course. Anyway, I've got another eye, haven't I? I haven't? Not after you've finished, wiping your feet on my face? Terrific, Dennis. What's that? Why am I making such a funny noise? Just a death-rattle, Dennis – it'll be over any second."

"Knowing Dennis" Georgie added, "he'll see you get a good Christian burial, too. Down the nearest drainhole."

"Dennis isn't that tough," Tim said. "That's what *you*

reckoned a little while ago, Leroy."

"Yeah, before Becca booted his machine. Now he *is* that tough."

Tim shook his head thoughtfully.

"I'm not so sure. I know Dennis is hard to like but maybe that's because of the way he looks. Haven't you seen people shudder at the sight of him? Maybe he's a bully as a sort of defence against being ugly – so he can tell himself he's *making* kids hate him, that he's in control of it. The trouble is when he behaves like that they hate him even more which makes him feel even uglier. It's a kind of vicious circle."

"What are we supposed to do about it?" Georgie asked.

"Like I said. Someone's got to break the circle. For a start by convincing Dennis he can be as popular as anyone else. Then maybe he'll begin to treat people better."

"Yeah, maybe," said Leroy. "Seems to me there are a lot of maybes in what you're saying, Tim. A kid could get murdered by all those maybes."

"It'll be dark soon," Georgie said hastily. He was trying to change the subject. When Tim went all holy like this it was very embarrassing to have him as your gang-leader.

"Wonder if Becca's got away," said Leroy.

"Must have. If she'd been caught her screams would reach us here on the Point. Are you sure there's nothing we can do, Tim?"

Tim nodded and they knew he was right. By now Sharon would have made sure Becca was well-hidden. Sometimes it seemed to Leroy and Georgie that Sharon was their real leader. Or even Becca herself who was a bit stuck-up but at least *did* things. When they looked at each other now, Leroy and Georgie – or was it Georgie and Leroy? – both knew they were wishing the same thing: if only Tim would get over his illness. This was embarrassing too.

"It's getting colder," Leroy shivered. "All of a sudden."

34

"Funny time of year this," said Georgie.

"It's Spring," said Tim. "There are leaves on the trees already, if you look. And did you see all the catkins and pussy-willows the little kids brought into school this week? Smashing. I like Spring."

He'd said the same thing about Winter. These days Tim seemed determined to like everything. Even Dennis Dogsmuck.

"And soon it'll be the Spring Fayre," Leroy said.

"Yeah," said Georgie.

"The Spring Fayre," murmured Tim.

According to some kids the Spring Fayre was better than your birthday, or even Christmas. It spread over the far side of the Heath and into the village where every shopfront, lampstandard and telegraph pole was hung with bunting and pennants. Beneath these, Sharon reckoned, everything was magic just like in the olden days: here you'd come across a fortune-teller, there a coconut-shy and everywhere you were invited to roll a penny, smash the crockery, knock over the skittles, guess the weight of the cake and generally try out your strength, your skill and your luck. Up on the Heath itself was a full-scale funfair that offered about a dozen different ways to make you sick. And in the evening there were fireworks. The closer the Spring Fayre got the more it seemed to take its time coming – yet always it seemed to be over in a twinkling.

"Last year was the best Spring Fayre ever," Leroy said.

"You reckoned that about the year before," said Georgie.

"No, last year was *special*."

They all nodded, knowing why.

"It'll be the same this year," Tim said.

"For the kids with bikes," agreed Georgie and Leroy.

Bikes. One word, five letters. Enough to tell you straight-away what was special about last year's Spring Fayre. They grinned as they remembered it

Tim was thinking about the Dips. The Dips were the oldest part of the Heath – the part that hadn't been smoothed over by the Council. Here were the hollows where gipsies used to camp when Mr Amos was a young shaver. Or so he said. They'd root up the heather and gorse-bushes and use the thin, scrunty trees for firewood. Mr Amos also said that in the time of his own great-great-grandfather, the Dips had sheltered highwaymen. Even today a rumour would sometimes spread through the school that a kid had come across a fossilised hoofprint in the Dips or found a chunk of flintlock pistol. All nonsense, of course, though easy to believe on mornings when the Heath was thick with mist. But ever since last year the Dips had been searched for a different sort of trophy.

"Here," a girl would say, "found it in the Dips."

"What is it?"

"What is it? A brake-block, of course. From the Contest."

"The Contest? How d'you know that? Could've come off a bike anytime."

"It's from the Contest, definitely. Got it from under the bush where they had to make that sharp turn. Probably it's from the bike that went out of control. Remember that?"

"Couldn't forget it, could I? No one could forget a crash like that."

"Well, this brake-block came from the bike. Definite, that is."

And the brake-block would change hands like some rare treasure. At other times the trophy was a piece of chain or a wheel-spoke or some badge or ornament. Whatever it was, its claim to fame was that it came from the Contest.

Leroy and Georgie were thinking about the Contest itself. It was the first ever rough-riding bike contest to be held at the Spring Fayre – or anywhere else so far as they knew. To win you had to be a safe cyclist as well as a skilful one because first came the Preliminary: two judges examined every bike and every rider for what they called roadworthiness. Points were awarded for how well your bike was looked after and how well you looked after other people, too, by knowing all about cycle-maintenance and safety, and the highway code. You could answer either ten straightforward questions, each worth a mark, or two really tough questions carrying five marks each. Everyone chose the straightforward questions, naturally. Even the laziest, dimmest kids slaved to pass the Prelim because only those with the highest scores were allowed to enter the Time-Trial.

The Time-Trial was the real Contest. Each competitor was checked with a stopwatch over the Dips at their worst – up and down a winding breakneck of a trackway, easing through obstacles that lost you a point if you touched them or if you put down a foot, across a waterjump, under a tunnel of branches, along a twenty-metre stretch of planking suspended six inches above thick mud and finishing with a slope so steep you almost had to bend your bike in half to get round its hairpin bends.

"The Time-Trial was fantastic," said Georgie.

Leroy nodded.

"Sure it was."

"Except who won it," said Tim. "The only bad thing about the whole Contest was who won it."

"Dennis was bound to win, wasn't he?" Georgie sniffed. "What with his Gents keeping the other kids away from the Dips so he was the only one who could practise. And he's been doing the same this year."

"Plus he's got a new bike this year," Leroy added. "Along with all the rest of his gang just about. That's sure to help his training. Also this is the last year he *can* win it – next year he'll be thirteen and too old to enter. He'll die rather than

37

lose."

"You mean other kids will die so he can win," said Georgie. "Remember what happened to his closest rival last year? That bike practically fell apart."

"No one could prove Dennis fixed that," Tim said.

"Sure they couldn't. And the kid was too scared to complain."

Tim shook his head.

"I still say it's wrong to try to out-thug Dennis. No one could be a bigger bully than him so why even try? There's got to be a better way."

"So you told us," said Georgie. "Sort of kissy-kissy Denny-wenny."

"I didn't say that."

"Sounded like it."

"Did it?"

When Tim's voice went gritty they knew why Dennis still treated him as their leader. This time it was Leroy who changed the subject.

"Wouldn't it be terrific," he said, "if one of us beat Dennis in the Contest!"

"Fat chance," said Georgie. "I'd settle for getting to the blinkin' starting line. Are you sure your Mum and Dad won't get you a bike, Tim?"

"As soon as I'm better. Not till then."

"And Becca's Mum still thinks she should be riding a scooter," Leroy said. "Or maybe a tricycle. And our Mum and Dad say they'll buy the five of us a bike each – the instant they've won the pools. So it looks like we're stuck with watching again."

"Great," said Georgie bitterly.

Even Tim sighed. He turned away and stared through the railings out over the back gardens. So he was the first to see the Miracle.

"Look!" he exclaimed.

Georgie and Leroy swung round.

The bikes were even more dazzling than before. Their metalwork glittered. Their paintwork flashed. And they jumped over fence after fence in a mad steeplechase as if this were a backyard Grand National.

"I don't believe it," gasped Georgie. "Bikes can't do that!"

"Especially when no one's riding them."

Wide-eyed, they watched as the runaway bikes reached the garden immediately below. Here, in a swishing, clicking jostle of colour, they slowed, circled once only and collapsed in a heap. A few wheels went on spinning for a while. A few handlebars twitched. Then all was still.

"I just don't believe it," said Georgie again. "Bikes acting like racehorses – all on their own?"

Leroy shrugged.

"There they are in front of you – Madboy's bike, Hogan Wade's bike, even Dennis's bike. All of them belonging to the Doggerty gang."

"Not all of them," said Tim.

"What?"

Tim pointed to the left where one bike had kept going. Leroy and Georgie caught a glimpse of its saddle and its rear wheel before it dipped below the furthest wall. Now their eyes were wider than ever.

"Was that . . . ?" they asked.

"Must be. That's the only bike in existence which could still win the Contest for us – the best bike in the universe, Mr Amos called it. Did you hear the sound it was making?"

They nodded. They heard it still.

Swish-and-click, swish-and-click, swish-and-click.

¶ Six

"You really want to give it a try?" asked Mr Amos.

"Sure," said Tim.

"Definitely," Georgie and Leroy said.

"What about you two girls – are you in this?"

Sharon and Becca nodded.

"You're all mad," said Mr Amos.

But his eyes, behind his spectacles, had a mad glint too.

"Just how d'you reckon to go about it?" he went on. "That's what I'd like to know."

"Well," Tim began, "we . . . we kind of expected you to tell us that."

"Me? Why me?"

"Because you first suggested it. To Becca. Don't you remember?"

"Of course I remember. But I was joking, son. Oh, not about the Mustang Machine – I was dead serious about that. But tracking it down? Capturing it? Taming it and training it and riding it in the Contest against this Dennis Dogwhatsit? It's the nuttiest notion I ever heard."

Tim swallowed.

"But couldn't you just . . . sort of think about it?"

Mr Amos bent forward till his long, bony nose was almost brushing Tim's.

"Oh I could think about it," he said. "I've had a lifetime to think about it, son, give or take a couple of years. Not a day's gone by when I haven't kept an eye open for the Mustang Machine. I've even dreamed about it – woken up in the morning and found my legs knotted up with cramp from pedalling all night and my hands red raw from eight hours of gripping tight to them handlebars . . . yes, you can bet I've thought about it. But thinking about it and doing it aren't quite the same. Golly, no. What you lot want isn't difficult. It isn't even tricky. It's just plain, rotten *impossible*."

"It can't be," Tim insisted.

"Can't it? Take a little look, son."

Swivelling in his chair, Mr Amos reached behind him and lifted the grubby lace curtain at the window.

"Now, what do you see?"

They stared out into midnight. Close up was the shadowy clutter of Mr Amos's backyard, a rusting, mouldering re-minder of his rag-and-bone days. Further off was a black-ness of roofs and trees, though the Point looming over them was blacker still as if the line of streetlamps winding to the top was for decoration only.

"Eh? Speak up!"

"Nothing," said Tim. "Just night."

"Exactly. The Mustang Machine is out there somewhere but night is all you can see. And that's all it wants you to see, you mark my words. That there cycle is as slinky as they come. Why, it could be up above us right now – parked against me own chimney-stack – but we'd never know. Not if it didn't want us to know. One thing I have learnt over all these years and you'd better take notice of it . . . you don't catch sight of the Mustang Machine except when it allows you to. Got it? That's why this safari-notion of yours, if you don't mind me saying so, kids, is just three penny-worth of moonshine. It's laughable – or it would be if I didn't feel like blubbing my eyes out for you."

The old man let the curtain fall back into place. They were glad now he hadn't switched on the light. In the gloom of his back parlour they could pretend no one was upset.

41

Sharon sniffed, then blew her nose loudly in case they thought she was crying. Leroy and Georgie started to fidget. Tim bit his lip.

"Mr Amos?" said Becca.

"Yes?"

"Suppose it *wants* to be hunted by us."

"What?"

"Suppose . . . suppose it's got fed up with running wild, with being – what did you call it – a maverick bike? Suppose it's *looking* for someone to trap it and care for it and be its master."

"Or mistress," said Tim. "Are you thinking what I'm thinking, Becca?"

She nodded. "You see, Mr Amos, if what you say is true then hasn't it made pretty sure already that we've had a good look? First, it rescues Sharon as if it were a knight in shining mudguards. Second, it dumps all the other bikes practically under the boys' noses. Third, it deliberately wakes me up when it could've slipped away easy as wink. It's as if it were . . . well, *luring* us!"

"Right," said Sharon.

"Right," said Georgie.

"Dead right," said Leroy. "That's brill, Becca. Really brill."

"Or dead wrong," Becca said. "What do you reckon, Mr Amos?"

They waited so long for a reply they wondered if the old man had gone deaf on purpose as he sometimes did. Then they noticed he was trembling.

"What's the matter with him?" Sharon whispered.

"Are you all right, Mr Amos?" Georgie asked.

The old man seemed to be having trouble with his breathing now. Like a horse at a trough he snorted and snuffled. His eyes were watering too.

"It must be some kind of attack," said Leroy. "Should we

42

fetch someone?"

"Don't bother," said Becca. "He's just laughing."

"Laughing?"

"He always gets like that. I'll have to slap him on the back in a second because he'll have started choking."

And a second later he had.

"Thank you, thank you," he spluttered. "Not quite so hard next time, Becca my dear. A couple of smart taps is good enough."

"Don't see what was so funny in the first place," said Sharon.

"Funny? Who said Becca's idea was funny? It was *happiness* that was making me laugh. You see she can't possibly have got it wrong. Nothing else makes sense! The Mustang Machine must be on the look-out for an owner – for some super-special person to be its first-and-last, one-and-only, now-or-never, famous-forever, ta-ra-and-boom-de-ay Rider! All my life I've been waiting for this – over seventy blinkin' years – and now finally it's happened! And you can take that look off your face, young Becca, because I'm not saying *I'm* going to be the rider. After all this time my bones are too old and my brain's too fuddled. But I'll bet a million quid to a milk-bottle top that one of you five sitting here will soon be the Master or Mistress of the Mustang Machine."

"One of us?" breathed Georgie.

"Are you sure?" Leroy gasped.

"I'm positive. Stands to reason, doesn't it?"

"Which one of us, I wonder?" exclaimed Sharon. "A twin? You, Becca? Me?"

"Or Tim?" added Becca, quickly.

Tim grinned wrily.

"Not me. Not in my condition. It'll be one of you four. But if it's going to happen it had better happen quickly

43

because it's less than a fortnight to the Fayre."

"Is it that soon?" said Mr Amos.

"The Fayre's a week away next Saturday."

"I see."

The old man turned back to the window.

"Dark as Newgate's knocker outside," he said, "give or take a few of them neon lamps. It's stopped raining now, too. Just about perfect conditions providing we're well wrapped up. Right, you lot. Follow me."

"Where are we going?" Sharon said.

But he was already shuffling to the door. He led them into the yard, switching on the scullery light as they passed through so that it shone outside on his junk.

"We'll need a bit of basic equipment," he said. "Bare hands won't be enough for this job. Here, you twins cop hold of this."

"What is it?" Georgie asked. "An overgrown shopping bag?"

"It's a net, dimbo," said Leroy.

"Yeah, but what's it for?"

"To catch a big two-wheeled fish," said Mr Amos. "Those weights will help to hold it down. Sharon, Becca, you take a coil of rope each – I've got a couple here that are nicely lasso-length. Put your arms through the middle and hook them over your shoulders . . . that's right. I'll bring my clasp-knife."

"A clasp-knife?"

"For the branding, Becca."

"You mean . . . the hunt starts now? Right away?"

"Why not?"

"But what if it goes on all night?"

"So you sleep late tomorrow. It's Sunday, isn't it? And you can't be worried about your parents or you wouldn't have crept out this late in the first place. As long as you get back

44

before they wake up what difference does it make?"

"None at all I suppose," said Becca.

"Everybody ready, then? We'll start up in the alleyways – where Becca found the ruined stable. If that's not one of its hide-outs then I'm a double-dutchman."

"Mr Amos?" said Tim.

"Yes?"

"If . . . if you did listen down a chimney would you hear what was being said by people inside the house?"

"Wouldn't know, son. Can't actually say I've done it."

"Does it matter right now?" said Leroy.

"Oh yes," Tim said.

He pointed. In the light that spilled from the back door they saw at once why it mattered right now. Up the side of the house, matt-black on the brickwork, were the mudtracks of a bike.

"It must be!" exclaimed Sharon.

Mr Amos agreed.

"No doubt about it. There's just one machine I know that can climb a wall like a fly."

"Or come down a wall," Tim said. "Are those tyre-marks *to* the roof or *from* the roof?"

"Is that important?" Georgie asked .

"Sure," said Tim. "If you want to follow them."

¶ Seven

Above them were cloud-mountains backed by a scatter of stars. The perfect pitch for the Mustang Machine, Becca said. Any second you expected to glimpse it up there, a sky free-wheeler no bigger than a pinprick.

"Can't actually say I've ever seen it flying," said Mr Amos. "I mean, it hasn't got wings."

"Maybe it flaps its ears," Georgie said. "You know, like Dumbo the flying elephant."

"Ears?" said Leroy. "Who says it's got ears?"

"Must have. How else could it listen down chimneys?"

"Maybe it's wired for sound."

"Yeah, and rocket-propelled!"

"And maybe it's got tiny high-pressure suckers on its tyres so it can scale walls and ride upside-down, that sort of stuff."

"Probably it's got antennae, too, so it doesn't have to *see* objects, it just kind of beams off them like radar."

"Might have all of those things," said Mr Amos. "Or none of them. For the most part they weren't around when I was a kid . . . but the Mustang Machine was."

"It could've been invented by some mad Victorian scientist who was ahead of his time," Sharon suggested.

"Just about anything could be true of the Mustang Machine. There's a lot we don't know about that bike. Perhaps we'll never know it. How's the track, Tim?"

"Still clear, Mr Amos. It's laying a trail for us, I'm sure of that. Why else would it keep dodging up onto these walls and windows? If it stayed on the ground we'd never be able to follow it with all these puddles."

"It wants us to catch up with it, definitely," said Becca.

"More than likely," Mr Amos said. "But don't expect it to be easy when we do. You see, there's a bit of a problem here. When we do catch up with it, how do you reckon it's going to choose from among you for its boss? You want to know my opinion? My guess is that each of you is being tested. The one who shapes up best on this expedition gets to brand the bike."

After that they were silent for a while. Georgie and Leroy held onto the net more firmly than ever. Sharon and Becca gripped tightly to their coils of rope. Even Tim seemed to clutch at something in his pocket. It was Becca who noticed.

"What's that, Tim?" she asked.

"Oh, just something I picked up for luck from Mr Amos's junk. It may come in handy later."

"Get back! Under that arch! Quick!"

The shout from Mr Amos had them scuttling after him. Jabbed by each other's elbows, their toes trodden on, they shrank back into the darkness scarcely daring to breathe.

"Here it comes," he whispered.

So slowly that not a bead of rain was disturbed on its glittering bodywork, the police-car swished by. Its engine-note, like a murmur of law-and-order, law-and-order, law-and-order, faded into the night.

"A cop-car!" said Leroy. "Is that all? Why the panic?"

"You're kidding," Mr Amos said. "Just think about it! A cop-car means cop-shop if we're spotted carrying this lot. They'd reckon I was blinkin' Fagin branching out into burglary. Keep your eyes peeled for another one – or for anyone else come to that. If people are out this late then either they'll be suspicious of us or we should be suspicious of them."

"Let's hurry all the same," said Tim. "I'm pretty certain

we're getting closer."

But it's not easy to hurry when you're glancing over your shoulder, up and down and from side to side as well as a-head. Every dog-bark makes you jump. Every unexpected echo sends you skulking into the shadows. The worst moment is the scream of a siren speeding into the distance. You feel it's after *you*, just circling a bit before the final pounce.

"Where are we?" asked Sharon at last.

"Good question," said Tim.

The tyre-tracks had led them along pavements, across roads, down back-alleys and over gorse and grass and cobbles. Now they stood in the crook of a high wall with a bank of ivy on one side and on the other a looming, ink-black mansion.

"Isn't it . . ." Becca began.

"The Park?"

Becca nodded.

"It's the Park, Tim. This is the east wall of the Park – that side-entrance that almost nobody uses."

"Doesn't look like the Park," Leroy said.

"Don't suppose you've ever seen it before at this time of night," said Mr Amos.

"It's spooky," said Sharon. "If I were a ghost I'd haunt places like this."

"Thanks," said Georgie. "Really cheered me up, that has."

"Keep looking," Tim urged them.

"What for?"

"The tracks. They'll be here somewhere."

But not, it seemed, on the gravel which glistened all round them in the lamplight. Nor on the brickwork, nor amongst the leaves.

"It can't have given up on us," said Tim. "Not after leading us this far.

"It hasn't, kids!"

Mr Amos's voice, though still quavery, had a catch of excitement in it that made him sound like a big kid himself.

"On top of the wall. See it?"

And there it was.

The Mustang Machine was too much for them to take in all at once. Their eyes had to build it up like a jigsaw, piece by piece.

"Those mudflaps . . ."

"That flash gear-change . . ."

"Them there trimmings on the handgrips . . ."

"Get a load of that saddle . . ."

"Or the chaincase . . ."

"Or the handlebars . . ."

"Or the wheels . . . so sparkly."

"Just like I remember it," said Mr Amos. "It hasn't changed a bit."

"It's not Victorian though," Sharon declared. "It's more like . . . sort of . . . permanent."

She'd summed it up for all of them. Every detail of the Mustang Machine added up to an any-time-any-place-bike, a forever-and-ever-amen-bike.

"Listen to it," Georgie said.

Click.

"Is it moving?" Leroy asked.

Click-click-click.

"Don't go yet!" called Mr Amos.

"Follow it!" Sharon cried.

Swish-and-click, swish-and-click, swish-and-click.

With a flip of its back light, the Machine vanished over the wall. They heard it gathering speed over the wet turf on the other side. Sharon groaned.

"It was just teasing us. It led us here *on purpose*."

"Of course," said Tim. "How else would we have known that one of the park-keepers had slipped up . . . and left the gate unlocked."

"What?"

"Come over here."

Tim demonstrated. The ancient ironwork, which looked half from a palace and half from a prison, slid open without a creak.

"And once we're inside," said Mr Amos, "we're safe from the cops and everybody else – provided we're quiet. What did I tell you, kids? Cycles don't come any slinkier than this one."

"And parks don't come any darker," said Sharon nervously.

"They do," Tim said. "This is a city-park and it's never completely dark in a city. Look at the glow from the streetlights."

"That's just round the edges."

Sharon was right. How could a place so friendly by day look so much like enemy territory at night? As they moved over the grass their shadows reached out ahead of them to where the Park was blindfold-black.

"Keep close together," Sharon begged.

They already were – so close that when Mr Amos stopped in his tracks all five cannoned into him.

"Look," he said. "Just look."

To their left, at the foot of the slope, was the river with the vast huddle of the city dipping down to it. From here to the horizon they saw the cut-out shapes of trees and chimneys and churches and office-blocks, dark against dark, amongst the glitter of fat, electric stars. On the night-breeze came the far-off rasp of a ship's hooter.

"Magic," breathed Sharon.

"You said it, my dear. The best view in the world, I reckon. Forget all that picture-postcard stuff about mountains and forests and the seaside. Give me a living, breathing city every time. I like a bit of hustle and bustle on my doorstep."

"What's that light?" Tim asked.

"Which one, son? There's a million lights."

"No, not that way. Behind us – over by the bandstand."

"It's a headlamp," said Sharon.

"And it's actually *in* the bandstand," Becca said.

The Mustang Machine was gliding round and round as if parading in a circus-ring. Its beam caught the columns and ornamental railings a section at a time so that the bandstand itself seemed to rotate. Another trick, perhaps? What should they do now?

"Surround it," whispered Mr Amos. "Leroy and Georgie take the far side with the net, Becca go this side and you, Sharon, that side. Tim, you and me had better stay out of it. Now move up on it slowly and be ready for my signal. When that comes – charge! I want that net over it, ropes lashed round it, all of you on top of it and everyone holding on tight as super-glue. This time it won't get away."

"Wanna bet?" Georgie said.

"Shut up!" Sharon hissed. "You're licked before you start, you are. Ready, everyone? Let's go."

They crept forward on hands and knees through a screen of rose-bushes they could smell better than the could see. At last, scratched and snagged, they crouched just below platform-height. Was everyone in position?

Above them, the Machine circled on.

"Charge!" yelled Mr Amos.

Up and over the railings they scrambled. At once the headlamps went off. For the next sixty seconds it was like playing British Bulldog in a blacked-out Bedlam.

"Got it!" announced Becca.

"That's me, you clot!" Sharon yelped. "Stop winding that rope round me – what do you think I am, a cocoon?"

"It's in the net! It's in the net!" Leroy shouted. "And it's

51

fighting for its life! Ow! That hurt. Can I put the boot in, Mr Amos?"

"Do anything, son, just don't let it escape!" Mr Amos called.

"Aaagh! It kicked *me* back instead of *you*," shrieked Georgie. "Get stuck in, Leroy. It's up my end of the net now thrashing about like it's gone beserk – but I think I've got it! Yes, I've got it!"

"Yeah – also it's got my foot," Leroy added. "It's twisting my leg right up round my neck. Oooh! Ouch! Get it off, somebody!"

As suddenly as it had begun, the commotion was over. After a few groans and some panting for breath, there was silence.

"Everyone okay?" Mr Amos asked. "You've left the bike in good nick, I hope?"

"Perfect nick," sniffed Georgie.

"Hardly touched it," Leroy said.

"Eh? All that kerfuffle and you hardly touched it? Sounded like you kids were taking it apart."

"We were taking each other apart," said Becca.

Sharon giggled.

"Somehow the net got over Leroy and Georgie. We were fighting ourselves. The bike wasn't there even to start with."

"It was," said Tim, "to start with. But once it had caused enough chaos it left you to it."

"So where is it now?"

"See for yourself."

Amongst the shadows on the crest of the hill, the Mustang Machine was a sharper-edged shadow. It reared up, its headlamp spearing the night.

"It's laughing," said Becca.

"A bike?" said Leroy.

"Just shivering in a gust of wind, maybe," Georgie

suggested.

"Bikes don't shiver either," insisted his brother. "Not normally."

"Laughing *is* normal for this bike," Becca said.

As they watched, the front wheel seemed to paw at the air. Then the Mustang Machine pirouetted three times on its backwheel and vanished over the skyline.

"Blinkin' ballet is normal for this bike," said Mr Amos.

At the top of the slope they paused. Where were they being led now? Far below was the boating-lake and behind it the Museum, an outline of domes and colonnades that made the rest of the night seem drab.

"No sign of it," said Leroy.

"Probably a trap," said Georgie. "Strikes me it's not us hunting the Machine, it's the Machine hunting us."

"That's what I think," said Tim. "So we must trap the Machine first."

"How?"

"Using this, maybe."

Tim pulled something hard and round from his pocket. It glinted dully in the moonlight.

"What is it, son?"

"It's a bicycle-bell. I found it in your backyard, Mr Amos. I've got an idea – but we'll need to test it first. Georgie, Leroy, can you paddle a canoe in the dark?"

"Sure."

"On the boating-pond, Tim?"

"Right. That's if Mr Amos can get a canoe loose for us. At night they're all chained together."

"You bet I can, Tim. But why?"

"I want the twins to paddle to the dead-centre of the pond and then ring the bell once or twice. Just to see what happens. Could you two do it?"

"Simple," said Georgie.

53

"Just ring the bell?" said Leroy. "Nothing more?"

"That's all. It's only a try-out."

Georgie and Leroy glanced at each other and shrugged.

"Nothing to it," they said.

But when they stood at the pond's edge they weren't so sure. Moonlight gave every detail an abracadabra aspect: a blue-grey shiver of trees reflected in a grey-blue shiver of water. The canoes bobbed and bumped. Mr Amos opened his clasp-knife, knelt down and reached for the holding-chain. The blade twisted in a link.

SNAP!

"Your canoe, young sirs," he announced.

"In you get," said Tim. "Here's the bell. Remember, just a couple of rings when you get to the middle of the pond. Then wait and see. You'll have to use your hands to paddle back afterwards but we'll give you a shove-off now."

One heave sent the canoe slicing through the water. Silver ripples fanned out behind it. By the time it had stopped moving, the twins were part of the darkness, though not the stillness. Fumbling could be heard and muffled grumbles. At last came the bell.

It rang out with an odd, tinny note:

TIRRA-LING!

And again:

TIRRA-LING!

They held their breath. All round them was a hush of leaves, nothing more. Even the distant murmur of the traffic had died away.

"What are we waiting for?" hissed Sharon.

"Quiet," said Tim softly. "It's on its way."

"You reckon?"

"I know it."

Suddenly, they all knew it.

Swish-and-click, swish-and-click, swish-and-click.

Out of the night came the Mustang Machine. Its paint-work outshadowed the deepest shadow in the Park — so black, so sleek did it look they felt scruffy gawping at it. On the edge of the pond, it hesitated.

"Go on," Tim whispered. "Prove I'm right."

For a split second longer, the Machine perched. Then it dipped forward into the water with a splash so gentle it was scarcely a splash at all.

"Neat as blow-me-a-kiss," murmured Mr Amos.

"It's after the canoe," Becca said.

"It's after the bell," said Tim.

They could still see the handlebars and the saddle. Like the horns and spine of some deep-pond monster, these glided above the surface. They could also hear shuffling and a sharp word from where the canoe had drifted, which was where the Machine had now arrived.

"Georgie, Leroy — don't try anything!" Tim shouted. "What are you doing?"

Too late. Still clutching the net they were trying to cast, the twins — plus canoe — pitched over in the water.

"Aaaaagh!"

This splash was a real splash — a kerplunking, kapowing, kibosh of a splash. Its spray rattled in the branches overhead and the widening circles of the waves it made smacked hard against the rim of the pond.

"We're drowning!" Georgie spluttered.

"Stand up then," snapped Sharon. "It's only waist-deep."

"We can't," Leroy gulped. "The net's tangled round our legs."

Already Sharon was wading towards them. Dimly she could be seen ducking beneath the surface, wrenching and cutting her brothers loose, upturning the canoe, wading back to the shore.

"What a girl!" exclaimed Mr Amos.

"What a bike," breathed Becca. "It was laughing again – just before it disappeared behind the trees. It could've been shaking off the water, I suppose, but I'll swear it was *laughing*."

¶ Eight

Saying goodbye at the park-gate wasn't easy because Sharon and Georgie and Leroy knew they were saying goodbye to the Mustang Machine, too, at least as its owner.

"Ah-choo!"

"Thanks, Sharon," said Leroy. "You've made me more wet than the pond did."

"None of us would be wet at all if you and Georgie had done what Tim told you. You're both nut-cases. If the bike's already made a fool of us on dry land, how come you think you can beat it when you're afloat?"

"Well, it was all occupied with swimming, wasn't it? We thought we had the advantage – that we could sort of fish it out."

"From a *canoe*? You reckoned you could net it and drag it aboard a canoe? You'd have to be a genius fisherman to do that. You'd need blinkin' magic harpoons."

"It seemed worth a try at the time, Sharon. I mean, there it was right next to us all kind of glinty in the water. We thought . . ." Georgie shrugged and broke off.

"You thought you'd already been chosen, that's what you thought: Mustang-Master Georgie and Mustang-Master Leroy, the twin trick-cyclists. Instead it's mouldy Georgie and mouldy Leroy and sopping-wet Sharon. Terrific, I must say."

"Don't keep on about it, sis," mumbled Leroy. "We're sorry, aren't we?"

"What?"

"We're . . . you know . . . sorry."

"Well that's one miracle tonight, anyway. Never thought I'd hear you apologising to me. For our next miracle let's see if we can get home without catching pneumonia – not to mention a good hiding from Mum and Dad. Cheers, Mr Amos. Cheers, you two. And good luck."

"Cheery-bye."

"See you."

"See you."

Standing there in the lamplight, Becca and Tim didn't seem much like a Mustang-Mistress or Mustang-Master, either: a prissy-looking girl with pigtails and a boy so thin his own breathing made him shake. They watched until the twins and their sister had given their last, bedraggled wave.

"Where now?" Becca asked. "Can we still pick up the trail, Tim?"

"We don't need to. We've got the bell. So we'll let the Mustang Machine pick us up."

"And if I'm not very much mistaken," said Mr Amos, "we've also now got the second half of your plan. What happened down there in the pond was what you expected, wasn't it?"

Tim grinned.

"Not the last bit. I'd rather have the others still with us. In fact, I'm not sure the three of us will be enough to carry out my idea."

"But you still think we've got a pretty good chance?"

"Let's say fair," said Tim.

"Will someone kindly tell me what the idea is?" Becca protested.

"We'll do better than that. We'll show you."

Tim lifted the bicycle-bell and rang it.

TIRRA-LING!

Just three more times he rang it: once on the main road

which ran alongside the Museum's north face; once again in the quiet avenue to the east of the naval college.

Tirra-Ling!

Tirra-Ling!

The third time was beside the river. Or what was left of the river.

"The tide's out," said Becca.

"I know."

"You say that as if it's part of your plan."

"It is."

Becca gazed across the flat wastes of the river-bed. Not even the moon could bring glamour to mud like this. Scattered about were half-submerged objects – old tyres, a milk-crate, driftwood. There was even a dustbin-lid sinking into the ooze. With the tide in, the river was the perfect frontage for the handsome college buildings – a lawn of high water. When the tide was out, it was no better than a rubbish-dump. So how could it be part of the plan?

"Listen!" Tim said.

"The bike?" whispered Mr Amos.

Tim lifted a finger to his lips. Eventually he shook his head.

"Not the one we're after anyway. Wait! There it is again."

For three full minutes they strained their ears for the faintest click, the slightest swish.

"Can't hear a dicky-bird," Mr Amos said.

"Nor me," said Becca.

Tim frowned.

"There was something there, definitely. But not from the direction I reckoned on. It should have been coming from over –"

Becca and Mr Amos swung round to where Tim had frozen in mid-point.

By now they ought to have got used to the Mustang

59

Machine. But how do you get used to such streamlining, such hairs-breadth balance? On the very brink of the quay, the best bike in the universe was poised as if for a kill.

"Ah . . ." sighed Tim.

And he raised the bell.

Tirra-Ling!

Before its sound had died away, he sent the bell spinning through the air. It plopped in the mud no more than a dozen feet from the flight of steps where they stood. At once the Machine plummeted after it.

Agog, they stared at the rearing, plunging fuss of what happened next. It was the energy of the Machine, not its weight, that got it into trouble. Every swerve and lunge drove it further into the ooze. Dollops of mess were flung in the air as it ploughed mad furrows over the riverbed. But all its frenzy was in vain: the harder it bucked the more the gunge sucked.

"It's not laughing now," Becca said.

"It's weakening," said Mr Amos. "Won't last much longer."

Nor did it. With a final twang of its spokes, the sog-smothered bike came to rest.

"Tim," Becca asked, "what do we do now?"

"We kneel in the mud, legs apart to spread our weight, and we dig it out with our hands."

"But then it'll monkey us about all over again, won't it?"

"Not if we've roped both wheels to its frame. It may be able to fly with the greatest of ease over any surface – except a riverbed, of course – but no bike can move a centimetre if its wheels won't go round. After that we carry it home."

"So simple!"

"When you know how, love," said Mr Amos. "But it takes a Tim to know how."

The riverbed was firmer than they expected but this meant it was harder to claw the Machine free. Halfway-to-finished, Tim stopped them.

"Okay," he said. "Now we must lash it up tight. This rope is thick enough to hold it, I think. For long enough to carry it to Mr Amos's, anyway. Your place all right for a corral, Mr Amos?"

"Sure, son. It'll be the most welcome lodger I've ever had and that's a fact!"

"Suppose it breaks out?"

"Eh? Look, Becca, my little old end-of-terrace may have seen better days but it's not that tumbledown. This here vehicle rides *over* walls, not through them. If we're careful, and crafty, it'll stay caught. You depend on it."

Certainly the Machine seemed harmless enough now. They eased it loose and lifted it – Becca at one end, Mr Amos and Tim at the other – up the steps to the cobbled waterfront.

"It stinks," said Becca.

"So do you. You're covered in mud as well."

"How will we get it off?"

"Hosepipe," said Mr Amos.

"Sorry?"

"We'll hose it down in the backyard. Soon be sparkling fresh again."

"I meant *me*."

"Oh. Won't your clothes clean up in the wash, my dear?"

"Not without Mum noticing."

Becca sighed. Still, wasn't it worth a row with Mum to have helped with such an adventure?

"Ready?" said Mr Amos. "Now for the greatest moment of my long, loopy life: the branding of the Mustang Machine. Just one carved initial on the frame should do it. Here you are, Tim, the sharpest blade on my clasp-knife. Two quick strokes and the best bike in the universe is yours."

"No, not mine."

61

"Not yours?

"It's got to be Becca."

"Me?" Becca gasped.

"It was your plan that worked, son. Without you, we'd have been led a dance all night."

"It was teamwork that did it," said Tim. "Besides . . ."

"Besides what?" asked Mr Amos gently.

"Well, it's not just a question of trapping the Machine, is it? It's also got to be ridden in the Contest and I'm not . . . fit enough. See?"

"But Tim –"

"Take the knife, love. He's right."

"So . . . so I'd have to ride in the Contest?"

"If you're willing."

Becca bit her lip. She was willing but was it right? Not Sharon, not Leroy, not Georgie, *her*.

"A letter B, Becca," said Tim. "That's all it takes."

"Okay."

The knife was so sharp she might have been scraping away ordinary paintwork on a nothing-special bike: B.

"Done it!" said Mr Amos, then stiffened suddenly. "Did you two hear that? Just like before – another bike by the sound of it. Maybe more than one."

"Let's get going," said Tim. "Other bikes don't matter now."

For once Tim was wrong. After they'd disappeared into the avenue with their trussed-up burden, two riders slid out from the waterfront shadows. Even by night there was something slimy about the taller of them. He sat back in the saddle flexing his fingers so that one second his glove made a fist, the next a claw.

"Now what do you make of that, Madboy?" he said. "I don't understand it at all. No, not at all do I understand it. And when I don't understand something, it makes me nervous."

"I've noticed that, Dennis."

"You have? Then kindly tell me what's going on."

"I dunno."

Dennis leant forward and prodded his companion's chest.

"You dunno? But you are my first lieutenant, aren't you? Which means it's your job to know. So if I may make a suggestion, my mad-little-bogey-boy . . ."

"Yes, Dennis?"

". . . you'd better naffin' find out."

¶ Nine

Madboy peered over the edge of the garage roof in the Sunday afternoon quiet.

"Perfect," he said. "We can see everything."

"Can we hear them, too?" asked Weasel Bates.

Madboy nodded.

"Bound to, this close. From here we could practically wipe their noses for them."

"Be good practice," said Weasel.

"Huh?"

"For when we have to do it for Dennis."

"What's that supposed to mean?"

"Well, we do everything else for Dennis, don't we? We fetch and carry for him, we polish his bike, we do his repairs. Stands to reason we'll end up wiping his nose. You know what the other kids call us?"

"Tell me."

"Dogsmuck's dogsbodies."

"Not when Dennis is around, they don't. Anyway, you objecting?"

Weasel considered it.

"Yeah. Reckon I am."

"You?" sneered Madboy. "Dennis only has to hiccough and you snap to attention. One word from Dennis and you'd pitch a tent on a level crossing – and then thank him very much for finding you a nice, flat site."

"Hark who's talking," Weasel said. "Haven't exactly noticed you standing up to Dennis."

"Can't."

"Why not?"

"If I stood up to Dennis the ponk would kill me."

"I'll tell him you said that."

"No, you won't. 'Cos he'd kill you first. Just like he's going to kill this Becca kid."

That reminded them. They turned their gaze back to Mr Amos's yard. The junk there had been cleared away, leaving an arena the size of a boxing-ring.

"I still don't get it," said Weasel.

"What?"

"The net. Why stretch a net across the tops of the walls like that? Turns it into a sort of cage."

"Must be trying to keep something in," said Madboy. "Or somebody out."

"What's old man Amos got that's worth pinching then?"

"Weasel, just use your eyes. Get a load of that bike in the corner for a start."

"That? All covered in gunge? Looks like an elephant's done job-jobs all over it."

Madboy shook his head wearily.

"What a crumbling Nelly you are, Weasel. Take a good noss at the thing. Have you ever seen a bike like that – all swept-back and chunky like a fighter-plane? It's got style, that has. You clean it up a bit and you've got yourself a nifty machine, I bet."

"Where's it come from?"

"Out of a blinkin' cornflake packet, I expect. How should I know?"

Conversation ceased for a while. Now and again they wriggled uncomfortably or glanced up at the sky which was heavy with rain to come. But not too soon, they hoped, because they daren't leave till they had something to tell

65

Dennis.

Suddenly Madboy stiffened.

"Watch it!" he hissed. "They're coming out."

"What's that they're carrying?" Weasel whispered.

It was straw mostly. Bales of it.

"Spread it out, kids," said Mr Amos. "Make a nice, spongy carpet of it all over. Then we'll fetch the mattresses. After that, Becca will have to take her chances."

Twenty minutes later, the yard was covered and the two spies on the garage roof had cramp.

"What's it all in aid of, Madboy?" Weasel groaned.

"Dunno. And keep your voice down or they'll spot us."

"Can't help it," yelped Weasel, "I'm in agony."

"Shut up, you goon!"

Below them, Tim swung round.

"Did you hear something?" he asked. "A sort of moan?"

"Probably me, son. All this exercise is beginning to catch up with me."

"No. . . it wasn't you, Mr Amos."

"Wasn't me either," snuffled Sharon. "Though this cold is something to moan about. Typical, I must say, when Georgie and Leroy haven't so much as sneezed!"

"We're just tough, sis," Leroy grinned. "Shall we fetch Becca?"

"Okay," said Tim. "But check her padding first. We can't afford any injuries."

"Right," Georgie said. "She is our number one rider. Not to mention our number two rider, our number three rider and our number four rider."

"Without young Becca, kids, it's goodbye to that Contest," said Mr Amos. "We'd better get the Machine set up for her. Sharon, you and Tim fetch it to the middle here – and keep stroking it, keep soothing it. Remember it's as wild as a tiger and just as dangerous!"

"But Becca's initial is on it," said Sharon. "She's its mistress."

"I know that," Mr Amos said, "and you know that. But does the Machine know that?"

"You mean it might resist?"

The old man eyed it thoughtfully.

"Well, it looks harmless enough now – propped there like it hasn't got a twitch to its name. But if you ask me, once Becca gets a leg across that saddle it'll nip about like a hornet in a honeypot. She's got to tame it, break it in, bronco-bust it. Only then will it be safe for her to ride. And I'm thinking it's not going to give in without a fight."

Sharon and Tim approached the bike warily.

"Steady, girl," she murmured. "Easy does it."

"How do we know it's a girl?" asked Tim.

"How do we know it's a boy?"

Tim laughed.

"Fair enough. Come on now, my lady . . . easy now . . . nothing to worry about . . . that's a good girl . . ."

Lightly, coaxingly, he ran his fingers along the handlebars. Sharon tickled the saddle on top and underneath. The bike didn't move.

"There's a beauty . . . there's an old softy cycle . . ."

"Don't fret now, it's all right . . ."

Still the bike didn't move. They glanced at each other

"Shall we?" Tim asked.

Sharon pulled a face.

"Why not?"

When they straightened the Machine up and wheeled it to the centre of the yard, no click or swish could have been sweeter.

"Nothing to it," said Sharon.

"Don't stop," Tim warned her. "Keep fussing over it."

"What's the point?"

"Two points actually, Sharon. For a start it's staying upright on its own – without a stand. And for a finish, feel the bodywork. Warm, isn't it? Just like flesh and blood."

"Cripes!"

"Easy my princess. Take it easy now . . ."

"Yeah, bike – take it easy!" Sharon yelped.

She patted the rear mudflap. Tim caressed the front.

Up on the roof, Weasel shook his head in bewilderment, his eyes and mouth agape.

"They're round the twist," he whispered. "Stark, staring bonkers."

"Keep looking," snapped Madboy. "And keep quiet."

"But they're barmy, I tell you. They're doodle-alley."

"Yeah . . . maybe."

"Maybe? What do you mean maybe? When did you last chat up a saddlebag?"

"Just watch."

"Who needs to? It's the nuthouse for this lot – definite. So why . . ." Weasel's voice trailed away. There were no words for what he saw next.

Becca was padded wherever padding could be held in place – round her arms, round her legs, round her body. And over every padded joint was more padding still: ankle-pads and knee-pads and elbow-pads. Her feet were padded, she had padded gloves and on her head was a padded helmet. Covering all this she wore a padded jump-suit much too big for her.

"Enter the human tea-cosy," Leroy announced.

"She looks like a suit of armour lagged for the winter!" exclaimed Georgie.

"And every ounce of it will come in handy," said Mr Amos. "You wait and see."

"How are you feeling, Becca?" Tim asked.

"Scared."

"So would I be."

"You would?"

"I'd be petrified. But also I'd be excited. Aren't you – a little bit?"

Becca nodded.

"A little bit. Mostly scared, though."

"Let's get on with it then. Georgie, Leroy, help her into the saddle. Sharon, you and me had better keep holding the bike till she's ready. Once she is, stand well clear. Tell us when, Becca."

"Okay."

Soon Becca was mounted, her feet poised on the pedals, her fingers tight round the hand-grips. She licked her lips. If she failed now the hopes of six people would be shattered. Did she dare?

At first her voice was no more than a croak. She had to say it again.

"Ready!"

The twins and Sharon scampered aside. Last to move was Tim. He let go slowly, his arms outstretched as he backed away. Becca held her breath. Georgie, Leroy, Sharon, Tim and Mr Amos held their breath. Even Madboy and Weasel held their breath.

Nothing happened.

Weasel pulled himself together.

"It's a joke," he insisted. "They've seen us up here and they're having us on."

"Shush."

"Shush yourself. I've had enough of this pantomime. What are we supposed to be waiting for – the blinkin' bike to turn a somersault? You'll be telling me next it can go . . ."

". . . backwards?" gasped Madboy.

"Backwards?" Sharon exclaimed. "Why are you riding backwards, Becca?"

"I'm not!" Becca cried. "That's the way it's taking me!"

Click-and-swish, click-and-swish, click-and-swish went the Mustang Machine. Round and round it swung like a coin spinning itself up on end instead of down flat.

"I'm getting dizzy!" yelled Becca. "Stop!"

At once the Machine stopped dead.

"Aaaaagh!"

Becca's feet flipped over her head and she bounced bottom-first on the straw.

"Nice one, cycle," said Mr Amos.

"You all right, Becca?" Tim asked.

"Fine."

Red-faced, gritting her teeth, Becca re-mounted.

This time the Machine threw her in slow motion. In a gradual tilt forward on its front wheel, it hoisted its back wheel up and over in the air, till she slithered off rather than fell. She was back on her feet and back on the bike straight-away.

"Okay, you brute. Try to get rid of me now."

With her arms she hugged the handlebars, with her legs she clamped the frame. Her mount reared and bucked and twirled in a sudden kangaroo-leap that hurled Becca into the ceiling of net. Like a spider on a web, she hung there a moment before lowering herself back to the yard's cluttered floor.

"Have a breather," suggested Mr Amos.

"No. I'll lose my nerve."

Attempt number four was the most spectacular yet. Every part of Becca, from her toes to her eyebrows, seemed to cling to the Machine – and every part was needed. How else could she have stayed on it as it whirled round the outside edge of the yard then suddenly – as if at a funfair wall of death – actually swung up onto the brickwork so she was riding parallel with the ground? But this wall was square, not circular.

At each of the four corners the Machine changed direction by hopping from one stretch to another and it was the tenth of these hops which unseated Becca. With a yell that must have been heard up on the Point, she crashlanded, rolled over twice and lay spread-eagled.

"Is . . . is she unconscious?" Sharon asked.

"Let's look," said Tim. "Keep away, Georgie. And you, Leroy. If she's hurt she'll want plenty of air."

They bent over Becca, afraid of what they'd find.

She was wide awake and scowling with anger. Pushing them aside, she sat up.

"That's it," she said. "That is *it*!"

Her glare at the Machine was enough to blister its paintwork. It was leaning in the corner of the yard where they'd first left it, as if nothing at all had happened.

"Scoop up all this straw," rapped Becca. "Get rid of these mattresses."

"Right inside the house?" asked Sharon.

"I want the ground completely clear."

Hands on hips, Becca watched as they did it, then she took off her helmet and gloves and unzipped the jumpsuit. Once she'd removed this, layer after layer of padding followed. Finally, in jeans and pullover, there was just Becca in the middle of the bare yard.

"It's a shame," said Mr Amos, "it's a crying shame."

"Shall I have a go?" Georgie offered.

"No, son. Becca's brand is on it and look what it did to her. It'd kill anyone else."

"She did her best, too," said Leroy. "Well done, Becca."

"You did great," Sharon sighed.

They looked at the Machine wistfully.

"Maybe tomorrow . . ." said Tim. "I mean, when you're feeling better, Becca, maybe . . . maybe you could try again tomorrow?"

She stared at him, her eyes still furious.

"Tomorrow?"

"Or the day after, of course."

"Why tomorrow? Why not now?"

"Now? But you've just taken off all the protective gear."

"That's right. So I can see if this Machine of mine really is out to get me. While I'm swaddled in all that padding it can bounce me about as much as it likes, knowing I won't get hurt. Now it's got to choose."

"But . . . but suppose it chooses to splatter you?"

"Then I'll stay splattered. And you can release it. It'll *never* have an owner."

"No, Becca," pleaded Sharon. "You can't."

"Watch me."

"She's off her chump," said Mr Amos. "We mustn't let her do it. Grab hold of her somebody."

"Don't anyone touch me," said Becca.

Her voice was low but her face had the look she'd given Dennis. They could almost hear again the twang of her foot in his spokes.

"Can't you stop her, Tim?" Sharon begged.

Tim slowly shook his head.

"I'd rather tackle the bike," he grinned.

Becca turned to the Mustang Machine. Her plaits had come loose and one of her sneakers was undone. With brickwork all round her and flat earth beneath, she looked too small, too slight for what was to come. Until she spoke, that is.

"Now you listen to me. You allowed us to capture you, we know that. And you let me scrape the first letter of my name on you. So why all this fuss and bother about being ridden? You're mine, now. We're partners. Kindly act like a partner. Just notice that I'm not as muscly as an all-in wrestler, will you? Also I'm not protected in any way. If you want to break my bones and fracture my skull, go ahead. If it's my blood you're after, you can splash it all over the yard. But ask yourself this: what happens afterwards? Because afterwards my friends here won't want you any more. They'll let you go. Oh, you're handsome all right but bikes aren't built for beauty, they're for riding. And this is your last chance to be ridden and to help us beat that vile thug Dennis who for all I know might be out looking for me right now. That's all I'm going to say. Now it's up to you."

Becca stepped forward. She lifted the bike away from the wall and swung herself into the saddle.

"Tim," she said. "Think of something that nobody else in the world has ever managed to do on a bike."

"Simple," said Tim. "Ride up a flight of stairs."

Becca nodded.

"That's fine. I am about to do it. Open your back door, please, Mr Amos. I'll turn round on your top-landing and come straight back down again – without putting my foot down once because that loses a mark in the Contest. Okay, Mustang Machine? Our training together is about to begin . . . or not. The choice is yours."

"Hey, the bike's trembling," Sharon exclaimed.

"It's shaking like a leaf," said Georgie.

"It's a tantrum," Leroy said. "It's about to go mad."

"Wrong," said Tim.

"Completely wrong," Mr Amos agreed. "We've seen it before, kids, at least twice. That bike is laughing."

"Laughing?"

"Are you sure?"

"How can you tell?"

"Because when I have a good old chortle, my dears, I shake like a leaf myself. I'm doing it now!"

So he was. Soon they all were. They laughed as the Mustang Machine began to move. They laughed as they followed it up the stairs, especially when it made a turn on the top-landing far tighter than any in the Contest. They laughed again as it bib-bobbed back down, step by step. Becca was laughing loudest of all.

Out on the garage roof Madboy and Weasel still lay flat, their cramp forgotten. Only with the first drops of rain did they shift themselves. Hoarse with terror, Weasel cleared his throat.

"What . . . what we gonna tell Dennis, Madboy?"

"The truth."

"He'll never believe us."

"Oh, he'll believe us. Eventually."

"What'll happen then?"

Madboy passed a hand over his brow which was wet with more than the weather.

"Then, Weasel?" he said. "Then? Then we'd better start saying our prayers."

¶ Ten

First a fist and then a claw.

Fist and claw.

Fist . . .

Claw.

No one spoke. No one dared look away from the glove. When its fingers were hooked, they winced. When it clenched, they trembled.

Fist . . .

Claw.

Fist and claw.

From this, and from the clatter of rain on the slates, they were half in a panic, half in a trance. The story told by Madboy and Weasel didn't much matter. What mattered was Dennis's response to it. For five minutes now he'd kept the Gents waiting, each second ticked off by the smash and grab of his hand. Suddenly, he spoke.

"Spiky-spiders . . ." he said.

Madboy swallowed.

"What's that, Dennis?"

". . . is too good for her," Dennis went on. "Unless we use real spiders: like tarantulas and black-widows."

"Good idea, Dennis. Might be a bit difficult to get hold of, though."

"On the other hand we could try the elephant-walk – with real elephants."

"A sort of stampede, Dennis? T'riffic. Assuming there's some available, of course."

75

"Then again, we could smother her with a true-life python-the-ponk – followed by a waterfall-burial good enough for naffin' Tarzan himself."

"Like it, Dennis, like it. Er, where d'you reckon there's a waterfall . . ." Madboy's voice faded.

"Madboy," Dennis said, "I was joking."

"Eh? Oh, I see. Course you were, Dennis, course you were. Aha. Aha-ha-ha. Fantastic, your sense of humour, Dennis. Trust you to see the funny side of it!"

"The funny side of what, Madboy?"

"Well, you know. . .it. This Becca kid and her Machine."

"Funny? That's *funny*?"

"Er, no. No, Dennis. Not exactly funny, I wouldn't say. More like . . ."

"More like what?"

Madboy's mouth tried to wrap itself round words that wouldn't come.

"More like . . ." he began desperately, "more like . . . you know . . ."

"Yes?"

"More like . . . *not* funny, Dennis. More like . . . kind of . . . *serious*?"

Dennis nodded slowly as giving his okay to an execution.

"Ho, yes," he said. "This is serious all right. Here am I all set to win my second all-comers bike title on my brand-new, glittering, zapped-up vehicle and what have we got: a little dinky-do primary-school kid riding a puny little pedal-pusher that just happens to be *remote-controlled*."

"Remote-controlled, Dennis?"

"Well, what do you think it is, Madboy?"

"Didn't look remote-controlled to me."

"Then how did it look?"

"Sort of . . . alive."

"Alive?"

76

Dennis's lips twisted into a sneer as if the execution had been bungled before his very eyes.

"Madboy, I have doubts about you sometimes. Sometimes I really do have my doubts about you. If that bike is alive, kindly tell me what they feed it on. Eh?"

"Dunno, Dennis."

"So think then. Give it your undivided attention. Bring the full force of that towering intellect of yours to bear on the problem. Does it nibble nuts and bolts, possibly? Or gobble up gear-shifts? Is it perhaps a sucker of wheel-spokes, or a chomper, maybe, at the odd bicycle-chain? Do they fill up some trough with bits of old puncture-outfit and let it slurp to its heart's content? Let's have your considered opinion, Madboy – go on, don't be bashful. We are all agog for the clickety-click of your computer-like intelligence."

"Leave off, Dennis, can't you?" Madboy begged.

In a flash, Dennis had him by the throat.

"What did you say?"

Madboy made a sound somewhere between a choke and a sob as Dennis bent so far forward it was hard to tell where Doggerty ended and Sullivan began . . . or would have been but for the freckle-ish blotches. Only Dennis had these.

"Don't you ever tell me what to do, my son. Not never no-how. Get me?"

"Got you, Dennis," Madboy gasped.

"'Cos you are the toughest of my Gents, you are. Tougher than Weasel, Stevie, Hogan, any of them. But what you are *not* is tougher than me. Savvy?"

"S-Savvy, Dennis."

"So don't get any ideas you can't back up with muscle, right?"

"Right, Dennis."

The claw around Madboy's neck loosened its grip then became a fist with one finger jutting like a prong into Madboy's chest.

"What a relief to know we understand each other so good. That settles our little disagreement, wouldn't you say? Tell me about her bike, Madboy."

"It's remote-controlled, Dennis."

"Correct. It's remote-controlled. And that means it must have a delicate mechanism, am I right?"

"You must be, Dennis."

"Correct. And a delicate mechanism is easy to upset, yes?"

"Yes."

"Correct. What I like about you, Madboy, is you're so quick on the uptake. Now work this out, if you'd be so kind. How can you make doubly sure, triply sure, multiply sure, that you've upset a delicate mechanism?"

"Tamper with it, Dennis?"

"No, Madboy. Not tamper with it. If you just tamper with it then it's possible someone might be able to put it right again afterwards. What you must do is make certain no one can put it right again afterwards – not even in a million years of genius repair-work."

"How d'you do that?"

"Simple, my son. You get hold of the afore-mentioned delicate mechanism, you convey it to a place where you are not going to be interrupted, and then – with an axe, with an iron-bar, with a sledgehammer, with whatever blunt naffin' instrument is handy – you smash it to smithereens. To smithereens. Understand?"

"Now, Dennis?"

"Right now. Take as long as you like, but do it. Oh, and Madboy . . ."

"Yes, Dennis?"

"I shall be waiting for you."

"Here, Dennis?"

"Anything wrong with here, Madboy?"

78

Madboy ran a dry tongue over drier lips and looked a-round. It wasn't a pretty hideout, certainly. One karate-chop from Dennis and the whole stableyard would have crashed about their ears in a shower of slates and bricks and bird-droppings. True, they'd done their best to tidy up the only section that was solid but no one could get rid of that cat smell. The trouble was Dennis himself had discovered the place. That made it perfect.

"It's . . . it's just the bikes, Dennis. We have to walk them down the alleyway – bumping them on all those steps – and along this rough track here. Can't be doing them any good, can it Dennis? And what about your bike? We have to carry that all the way, don't we? It's got to be a waste of manpow-er, Dennis. I mean . . ." Madboy's words trailed away. Already he'd said too much. Beneath speckled half-hooded lids, Dennis's eyes glittered.

"A waste of manpower?" he said.

"Not a waste exactly, Dennis. I mean, it only involves about three Gents now I come to think about it –"

"I agree."

"What?"

"I agree, Madboy. It is a waste."

"It is?"

"Course it is. And it means the three of you then have to go back up all those steps, right to the top of the alleyway, to collect your own bikes. Every time. I never looked at it that way before. That's just what it is, Madboy: a waste of man-power. Thank you for pointing it out to me."

Dennis stretched out a hand and with the tips of his fin-gers only, patted his lieutenant's cheek. Blinking with relief, Madboy shrugged.

"That's all right, Dennis. It's – it's part of my job, isn't it?"

"It is, my son, it is. And thank you for volunteering."

"Volunteering?"

"To carry my bike in future by yourself. On your jack. Solo. I appreciate it, I really do. 'Cos it won't be easy on your own to make sure you don't bump a tyre or scratch the paintwork or even let a naffin' shadow fall across it. And if my bike doesn't arrive here in mint condition every time . . . you'll have me to answer to, won't you?"

"Mint condition, Dennis," said Madboy thickly. "Every time."

"You got it. Anything else, Madboy?"

"No, Dennis."

"Then why are you still standing here? By now you should be halfway there."

"But . . ."

"Yes?"

"Nothing, Dennis. Who shall I take with me?"

Slumping in the the broken manger, Dennis shifted into his thinking position. Again they all waited.

"This," he said eventually, "is a case for what you might call saturation-smashing. So take *everyone*, Madboy."

"Okay."

"Everyone . . . except Weasel, that is."

Weasel snapped upright.

"Not me, Dennis?"

"You stay with me, Weasel. I want a little chat. You see, there's gossip about you . . . little whispers that you aren't happy doing what I tell you. Just talk, of course. Must be just talk. But how did the talk start, I ask myself . . . that's what we've got to discuss. Assuming you're happy to stay, that is."

Weasel nodded dumbly.

"Of course, Dennis."

"Handsome," said Dennis. "Naffin' handsome."

Even before he and Weasel were alone, his left hand had slipped back into his favourite fidget: first a fist and then a claw.

¶ Eleven

It was raining again – in the village, on the heath, up at the Point and down by the river. Everywhere you could reach by walking, rain fell.

Especially rain fell at the Dips.

"Get a load of that trackway," Leroy said. "Looks like a tank has churned it up."

"The water-jump is worse," said Georgie. "You'd think it was a test-site for submarines. Plus the tunnel's gurgling away like a sewer, and the plank's floating on mud. The whole course is like a swamp."

"Smashing," declared Mr Amos. "Not even Dennis comes here on a day like this. It's what you might call one-bike weather: Mustang Machine weather!"

"How fast is she lapping now, Tim?" asked Sharon.

Tim glanced up from the stop-watch.

"Fifty-eight seconds," he said.

"How fast?"

"Two seconds under the minute. That's thirty-one seconds faster than Dennis's record last year."

"She's beating Dennis by more than half-a-minute . . . in these conditions?"

"So far, Sharon. And she's getting round quicker with every lap so there's a good chance she'll clip off a few seconds more before we finish the practice. Remember, too, Dennis lost a point when he had to put his foot down to keep his balance. Becca hasn't done that once, yet."

"She'll walk it," Leroy said.

"She won't," grinned Tim. "If she does that she'll lose a mark with every step. That's no way to win the Contest!"

"It's in the bag, I tell you," Mr Amos said. "An odds-on, twenty-two carat, one hundred per cent proof Dead Cert."

Tim frowned.

"Dennis isn't finished yet."

"Not by a long chalk," said Leroy. "Dennis knows every dirty trick in the book."

"If you ask me Dennis wrote the book," Georgie said. "Only he kept secret the worst couple of chapters to give himself the advantage. There's no telling what Dennis'll do next."

"You're so cheerful, you are," said Sharon. "What *can* he do? Send out some kamikaze-kids to duff up the Machine or die?"

"Wouldn't surprise me."

"Nor me," said Tim. "Dennis can't afford to lose. He's been showing off since Christmas with that new bike of his. If he's licked now by someone two years younger his reign of terror will be over. Everyone will know he doesn't always come out on top."

"Didn't you want to be nice to him once upon a time?" Leroy said.

"I still do. If he'd let me."

"Some hopes. Being nice to Dennis is like trying to Indian-wrestle with a gorilla: one handshake and you find your arm's torn off."

"There's only one way to deal with Dennis," said Mr Amos. "You've got to beat him fair and square in front of everybody even though he's broken every rule going. Tim's right, you know. Dennis can't afford to lose – ever. One failure and he'll be just like any other big kid, all mouth and trousers."

"Well I reckon he's bound to be beaten fair and square,"

Sharon said. "Just look at the way she's going!"

Tim clicked the stopwatch.

"Okay, Becca," he said. "Give it all you've got."

The girl and the bike were so much part of each other now it was hard to say which was doing the leading – Mustang Machine or Mustang Mistress. With a splash and scatter of puddles they plunged down the first of the slopes, swung over the first dip and skidded sideways into the first bend. Then came slope, dip and bend number two – only half as high but twice as hard because each moved *upwards* till pace and pedalling brought dip, slope and bend number three in a sudden downward swoop that threatened to send cycle and cyclist headlong into the water-jump. This jutted across the track the size and depth of a double-bath.

"Careful," Georgie breathed.

The Becca-Machine took the jump at a hop.

Next came the slow section: a figure of eight marked out by logs with an exit beneath a low cane. This had to be ducked under, limbo-style. Nifty as a sailor tying a knot, Mustang-Becca was through in a trice.

The tree tunnel followed – bushes hooked together in a long, winding coil that forced the rider to hunch low, hurtling eventually from the end of it like a slow bullet from a bent gun-barrel.

"Neat!" Leroy grinned.

The way they took the planking was neater. With its tyre-trail dead-centre behind it, the Becca-bike skimmed so fast over the surface the woodwork was hardly disturbed.

"Brill," murmured Sharon.

As brill as that zig-zagging, helter-skelter rush down the final slope?

"If your eyes didn't see it, your brain wouldn't believe it," Mr Amos said. "How fast was that lap, Tim?"

Tim shook his head slowly.

"My brain won't believe it," he said, "even though my eyes did see it. The stop-watch must be wrong. According to this thing she clocked . . ."

"Yes, son?"

"Tell us," Sharon begged.

Tim let out a long breath.

". . . fifty seconds dead," he said. "That's thirty-nine seconds better than Dennis's best: *thirty-nine seconds*. And through all this sludge and slush, too! She'd drop another four or five seconds at least if the ground were as hard as last year . . . which means she'd be travelling twice as fast as Dennis – two laps to his one."

"It's unbelievable," said Sharon.

"It's the Mustang-Machine," said Mr Amos. "Ridden by its rightful owner, the one kid in the world who can stay in its saddle."

"Well done, Becca," Tim said. "Fifty seconds that last lap."

Becca wiped the rain from the visor of her crash helmet. On the sleek machine with its glitter-black bodywork and wheels designed at the rear for a farm and at the front for a circus, she looked much too small. Or she would have done if she hadn't fitted the bike so snugly: Mistress of the Mustang Machine. Tim kept his eyes on the stopwatch.

"Easily enough to clobber Dennis in the Contest," he added.

"Really? I'm going to do it?"

"Do it?" exclaimed Mr Amos. "Riding like that you could win the Tour-de-blinkin'-France."

Becca sighed and patted the handlebars.

"I still wish it could have been you, Tim," she said.

"Well it couldn't so there's no point thinking about it. It's your initial on the bike, Becca, and it'll be your victory. What's it matter so long as we turn Dennis into a normal human being?"

84

"I suppose that is the important thing."

"It's the only thing," Tim insisted.

"Maybe," said Georgie, "but it's still a shame the rest of us can't have a ride."

"There's no point in thinking about that, either, unless you want to end up in plaster from head to foot. Mr Amos said it: Becca is the only kid in the world who can stay in that saddle for more than the time it takes to get catapulted straight out again. It's her brand . . . which makes it her bike."

"But if I do win, it'll be a victory for us all," Becca said. "Every kid we know will share in the prize – the finish of Dogsmuck Doggerty."

"Let's drink a toast," said Sharon suddenly.

She cupped her hands and held them up to the rain.

"All of us," she said.

It was Sharon and her magic again. But wasn't the Mustang Machine itself pure magic? They squelched into a circle and raised their cupped hands, too – three black kids, an old man white as Santa Claus, a boy so pale you felt he was too weak to lift his head from a pillow and a posh girl astride a posh bike. They waited for the raindrops to gather, then Sharon looked at Tim. He shook his head.

"Becca," he said. "You propose the toast."

"Me?"

"You . . . our leader."

No one spoke. They kept their eyes on the rain splashing in their fingers.

"Okay," said Becca.

But it was some while before she could do it.

"To the finish of Dogsmuck Doggerty."

"The finish of Dogsmuck Doggerty," everyone repeated.

They bent their heads to their hands and drank.

Afterwards, it was as if they had won the Contest already. They swanked across the Heath with Becca, their leader, in front, wheeling her Machine now so that Tim at the back could keep up. They turned their faces up to the sky and stuck out their tongues.

"It's champagne," Mr Amos declared, "the very best bubbly sent down to us by way of celebration: vintage cloud-juice, every drop. And you deserve it all, Becca."

"We all do. We're a team," Becca insisted.

"So we are – and I feel sorry for everyone who's not a member. Just think, kids, no one else in the world has got a share in the Mustang Machine except us. At the moment, anyway. Of course, one of these days it may get to be someone else's turn."

"You mean . . . the bike won't be ours forever?" Becca asked.

The old man shrugged and scratched his head so that a spike of wet, white hair stuck up like a question-mark.

"Who can say, Becca? It'll belong to us for long enough, I'm sure . . . just long enough. You see, while I was watching you on your practice laps back there I suddenly got a picture in my mind of the way it was that night by the river when you put your brand on it. It was dark so I can't be positive but I'm pretty certain you didn't carve your initials at all, not really. It was more a case of *uncovering* your initials. Don't ask me what we're supposed to make of that. Nothing at all, possibly. But deep down in my brittle old bones I can't help feeling that however much that bike is ours right now it's only on loan to us – the time'll come when we've got to give it back."

This thought made the Mustang Machine seem more special than ever. Becca coaxed it along like a jockey leading a thoroughbred with Georgie and Leroy on one side and Sharon with Mr Amos on the other. Behind them came Tim. Wet through and not caring a bit they trooped down into the village. Already every shop-front was hung with bunting and overhead the main street was criss-crossed with pennants. Every flag was in their honour, they felt, all rinsing nicely in the rain till Saturday when sunshine would spruce up the whole Spring Fayre. Up and out of the village they paraded, across the Point, flat as a horizon, and down again towards the terrace where Mr Amos lived. But before this came a shortcut through the disused railway tunnel where Tim had first glimpsed the Mustang Machine.

Here was where Madboy and the others lay in wait.

¶ Twelve

The time and place for the ambush were perfect. To right and left rose the railway embankment, its weeds, nettles and thorn bushes hissing with rain: no easy escape there. Nor was it easy to go back the way they had come – with the gravel and rotting sleepers of the track to slow them. Also they were thinking already about home.

"Oh for dry clothes," sniffled Sharon.

"And hot cocoa," said Mr Amos.

Becca lifted a hand.

"Not quite yet," she said.

Ahead of them, in the arch of the tunnel, stood Madboy. His face was full of a grin he had copied from Dennis.

"Wotcher," he said.

"Wotcher," called Stevie Spinks from the top of one slope.

"Wotcher," called Hogan Wade from the other.

Cutting off retreat, the rest of the Gents spread across the track behind them, all with the same grin.

"Wotcher," they said.

In their fists they held rocks and bricks. Their eyes were on the Machine.

"Like your bike," said Madboy. "Like it a lot."

"You leave us alone," Becca said.

Madboy sniggered.

"We intend to. We won't lay a finger on you – not a finger."

"So let us through," Becca said.

"Any time you like, little darlin'," said Madboy. "We won't

88

stop you. Or your mates. Right, Gents?"

"Right," said the Gents.

"What do you want then?" asked Becca.

Madboy tapped the flat of one hand with the crowbar he held in the other. Even the toss of his head was a passable imitation of Dennis's.

"Can't you guess?" he said.

"They're after the Machine," said Mr Amos.

"He's got it," said Madboy. "He's got it perfect. Full marks to the old geezer."

"But this bike's no use to you," Becca said.

"Not a bit of use," Madboy agreed, "being as how it's remote-controlled and all. But that's not what bothers us, darlin', the point being that it *is* of use to you. And Dennis doesn't like that. Especially he doesn't like it if you're thinking of entering for the Contest. He reckons that gives you an unfair start."

"An unfair start? That's a laugh coming from Dennis! Anyway, there's nothing remote-controlled about this bike."

"Really? Living and breathing is it? Feed it on bits of old puncture-outfit, do you? Give it a nightly bucket of nuts and bolts and stuff? We'd have to be mental to believe that. We've seen that bike in action, kid, so you can't fool us. It's remote-controlled all right. So kindly remote-control it over to me for a closer look, a very much closer look. In fact, me and the rest of the Gents here are going to do you a big favour. We're going to tune it up a bit for you."

"You'll wreck it!"

"Who, us?"

"Yes, you!"

"Temper, temper, kiddo. No need to get your knickers in a twist, 'cos you haven't got a lot of choice. Stevie, Hogan, show them how much choice they've got."

Stevie lifted his half-brick and Hogan his chunk of paving-stone. They bowled them overarm with a flick of the wrist as if they were playing cricket. Both missiles bounced once on the slope and spun across the track. The brick missed Becca only because she lurched backwards. The pavingstone shattered against a tree-root, one piece of it rattling against the front wheel of the Mustang Machine.

At once it began to move: swish-and-click, swish-and-click, swish-and-click.

"Now that's what I call sensible," said Madboy. "You can stop it right in the tunnel, our workshop as you might call it. That's where we do our tuning-up."

He stood aside as the bike passed him. It vanished into the gloom of the archway. Madboy signalled to Stevie and Hogan.

Follow me," he said. "The rest of you watch them."

"Can't we do something?" asked Sharon.

Becca bit her lip.

"Just leave it to the Machine," she said.

"But it's letting them get away with it."

"Don't you believe it," said Mr Amos.

He sounded far from confident, though. Why was the Machine following Madboy's instructions? Had Becca ridden it much too hard back at the Dips so that now it was too exhausted to resist? For a swish-less, click-less minute they waited.

Then, from the tunnel, came the clang of a crowbar against metalwork. Before the echo had died it was followed by other sounds – of rocks smashing into a chain-case, of wheels splintering under a hail of bricks. Afterwards came the crowbar again; They heard the crash-tinkle-tinkle of a shattered headlamp and the groan of burst saddle-springs.

"Just leave it to the Machine," said Sharon bitterly.

"Sounds like a great tune-up, Gents," remarked one of their guards. "Now don't you kids get any big ideas about rescuing that bike or we'll play the same tune on you: the death-march."

"Yeah, the death-march," giggled the others.

And they began to hum it, waving their rocks and bricks in time: DUM-DUM-DEE-DUM, DUM-DEE-DUM-DUM-DUM-DEE-DUM.

"Stand up straight," Becca snapped. "And keep your heads up. It's not a funeral yet."

"Isn't it?" said Sharon. "What's this then?"

Madboy, Stevie and Hogan certainly looked like a burial-party as they emerged from the archway. In their arms they held what had once been a jet-black bike.

"Oh dear," said Madboy. "I think we overdid it."

Smirking, he threw down a set of handlebars, battered shapeless. Stevie and Hogan followed with a main frame so bent and flattened that in comparison the crumpled wheels at either end of it looked almost workable – if you allowed for a couple of dozen broken spokes, a chain that hung loose and a pair of snapped-off pedals. Far worse than the damage itself, though, was the sparkle and polish of what was left: these were the remains of a brand-new bike. Madboy pretended to wipe away a tear.

"Naughty, naughty us," he said. "Never know when to stop that's our trouble. Feel free to have a good grizzle if it makes you feel better."

"Yeah," said a Gent, "feel free to blub."

"Why should we?" asked Becca.

Madboy blinked in surprise.

"You mean you like getting your machine smashed up?"

"No."

"So why aren't you crying?"

Becca shrugged.

"There's nothing to make us upset."

"How come?

"Simple. That's not our machine."

"Not your machine? Whose is it then, Dumbdumb?"

"No idea. Must be one of yours, I suppose."

"One of ours? How could it be one of ours? We left all our bikes at the top of the slope, see."

"Except yours, Madboy," Stevie pointed out. "You parked yours at the back of the tunnel, remember?"

"That's it then," said Becca. "They must've got swopped over in the tunnel. You've just bashed in your own bike – Dumbdumb."

Suddenly they were all looking at the crumpled metal on the track. Everyone except Madboy, that is. For a long moment he stood motionless, his smirk frozen on his face. Then, so slowly he seemed to be moving millimetre by millimetre, he knelt down to examine the wreckage.

"My bike," he whispered at last.

He lifted the crushed frame and tried to spin the front wheel. At once, in a jangle of spokes, it fell off.

"My bike . . . my beautiful bike."

"Feel free to have a good grizzle if it makes you feel better," said Leroy.

"Yeah," said Georgie, "feel free to blub."

"Never know when to stop that's your trouble," Sharon added.

It was almost her trouble, too. Madboy's look was no copy of Dennis's now. His teeth were bared with pure, original hate as he stood up, raising the crowbar above his head. Quickly Becca stepped in front of her gang.

It was the Mustang Machine – what else? – that saved her.

"Look!" Hogan called. "Up there on the bridge! There it is!"

Sleeker, more glistening than ever, it pranced on the very brink of the parapet, shaking off the rain.

"Get it!" snarled Madboy.

"What about them?" Stevie asked.

"They don't matter. I want that bike clobbered so hard it won't be worth a sniff from a rag-and-bone man. *Get it*!"

Already he was halfway up the slope ahead of them.

"They haven't got a chance," chuckled Mr Amos. "Wouldn't mind betting it'll be at home waiting for us by the time we get there. With a dry towel and a hot cup of cocoa ready for each of us, more than likely."

"Let's hope it's got out the bike books, too," Becca said, "and all our cleaning kit. Remember we haven't even got to the Time-Trial yet. First comes the Preliminary. We've got to make the Machine gleam all over – and spring-clean my brains, too, while we're at it. A couple of specks of rust or a couple of wrong answers and we're finished. Those judges only let the best kids and the best bikes enter."

"But we've *got* the best kid and the best bike," said Sharon.

"That's right," Mr Amos said. "With all the swotting you've done plus a little bit of last-minute spit-and-polish, that there Contest must be in the bag. Dennis Dogsmuck-Doggerty, or whatever your name is, sure as brake-blocks are brake-blocks, you've had it!"

"Did you say something, Tim?" Becca asked.

But before Tim could reply, Georgie and Leroy had started singing.

"Dennis Dogsmuck, Boo Hoo!
Dennis Dogsmuck – you're through!
Better give up in the Contest,
Becca's better than you!"

All the way back to Mr Amos's they sang it. Only Tim kept quiet . . . though none of them noticed this.

¶ Thirteen

"Question number ten," announced the judge. "Ready?"

Dennis yawned. He'd yawned between every question so far but that hadn't prevented him getting them all right.

"Never been anything else," he said.

"Why should high-rise handlebars never be fitted to a cycle with a diamond-shaped frame?"

"It mucks up the bike's steering. And its balance."

"Correct. That's ten out of ten for last year's champion."

Again it was the Gents in the front row who did most of the clapping. Apart from Tim, of course. Tim even clapped the kids who got an answer wrong. Dennis sucked at a tooth and took a long look at his watch to let everyone know that the Prelim was something he had to go through to reach the Time-Trial but otherwise wasn't worth bothering with.

"And while you've been sitting here, Dennis, my colleague has been examining your own cycle to check how well you look after it," the judge went on.

"He doesn't look after it," Sharon whispered. "The Gents do it all for him."

"He'll still get full marks," said Becca. "Just like last year."

Dennis had slouched to his feet.

"Yeah, well that's another ten out of ten," he shrugged. "Foregone conclusion."

"I'm afraid not," said the second judge.

"What?"

"You only score eight out of ten."

"Eight? Naffin' eight? How come?"

"The spokes in your front wheel are slightly out of alignment. They look as if they've been repaired recently in rather a hurry. Your cycle's not actually unsafe but by the very highest standards – our standards in this Contest – it's enough to lose you two marks."

"That gives you a total of eighteen out of twenty," the first judge said. "You still qualify for the Time-Trial . . . though only just."

"I only just qualify?" Dennis snarled. "Me? The reigning Champion?"

"That's right. Unless, of course, you argue with us. That would lose you a third mark and put you out of the competition . . ."

The first judge's pencil poised over his score sheet. From the look on his face it was clear he'd be only too pleased to ban Dennis. Both he and the second judge were big, burly ex-policemen and knew all about the Doggertys of this world.

Seeing Dennis control himself was like watching a volcano suck back all its lava.

"Argue?" he grated. "I never argue, mister."

"That's very sensible of you, Dennis. Who's next?"

Judge Number Two consulted his list.

"Young Becca," he said. "A newcomer. Our last entrant."

As Becca went up the steps to the stage, she passed Dennis coming down.

"Cremation?" he hissed. "Or old-fashioned burial?"

"Sorry?"

"Your funeral."

She hadn't time to answer. Judge One was already ushering her into the competitor's chair. He riffled through the question-cards.

"Now, Becca, ten questions to go."

"No," said Becca.

"Pardon?"

"Two questions, please. The five-mark questions."

Some kids gasped. Others whistled. Many slid to the edges of their chairs. The tough questions? So tricky that no one ever chose them? What was Becca playing at?

"Are you sure, young lady?" asked the judge. "They're worth a lot, I know, but you also stand to lose a lot. Won't that make you nervous?"

"I'm nervous already," Becca said. "Ten questions would drive me screwy. I'd rather chance the two."

"She's mad," Leroy groaned, "she'll blow it."

"Can't we stop her?" asked Georgie.

"Becca knows what she's doing," Tim said.

But did she? Clearly the judge had his doubts. He paused, as if expecting her to change her mind. When she didn't, he sighed.

"Your first five-mark question coming up then," he said. "Think carefully before you answer it. Ready? Now . . . in each case giving centimetres as well as inches, tell me the following measurements: the slack at the top that is reasonable for a cycle-chain in good condition; the approximate height from the ground that the centre of the bottom bracket spindle should be, for safety reasons; and finally the minimum length of handlebars stem that must remain inside the steering-head when it comes to brake-adjustment. I'll just repeat the question –"

"Please don't," Becca interrupted. "I'll get all jittery and freeze up. The first answer – for the chain – is about half-an-inch or 1.3 cm; the second is that the bracket-spindle should be approximately $9^1/_2$ inches or 24 centimetres from the ground at its centre; and thirdly you've got to leave at least $2^1/_2$ inches or 6.4 centimetres of handlebar stem inside the steering-head."

"All three answers absolutely correct!" beamed the judge. "Five marks!"

Through the crash of applause that followed, Becca sat tight-lipped. The eyes of every kid in the hall were on her, she knew, including the spite-filled eyes of Dennis. She knew, too, that Sharon's eyes would be crossed – plus her arms, her fingers, her legs and even her toes if she could manage it. Suppose the final question was just too difficult? Suppose the gang was let down now? Becca shuddered. Her tongue and the inside of her mouth felt as rough and cracked as toadskin. Her hands trembled. Relax, Becca, she told herself, relax.

"Quiet, please!" called the judge. "Everyone quiet now, please. Let the girl concentrate."

He nodded to Becca.

"Here is your second and final question," he said. "Take your time about it. Name all the parts of a bike that require lubrication – together with the two parts which you must be careful to keep clear of oil. Shall I –"

"No," said Becca. "Here goes: the two parts you must keep clear of oil are the brake rubbers and the wheel rims. The other bits which you've got to check regularly for lubrication are where metal rubs on brake mechanisms, the hinged joints on braked levers or rods, the head races, wheel hub bearings, bottom bracket bearings, pedal bearings, the chain and the free wheel and variable speed hub. But the last two need a thin oil, like sewing-machines, because thicker oil clogs up the –"

"Five marks!"

The clapping this time hurt their ears. Also it made Mr Amos sneeze. At least, that's how he explained the handkerchief that covered his face. Only Dennis and his Gents stayed still. The cheering in the hall went on till the second judge returned. He held up his score sheet to quiet them. At last the commotion died down.

"For care of her bike," he said, "Becca scores ten marks out of ten."

"Making a grand total of twenty out of twenty," said his colleague.

"*Two more than Dennis! Two more than Dennis!*", Sharon chanted.

Others began to chant with her: *Two more than Dennis, two more than Dennis, two more then Dennis, two more than Dennis!* Soon everyone was chanting. Or nearly everyone. The Doggerty Gents didn't join in and neither did Tim.

Two more than Dennis! Two more than Dennis!

Then came clapping in time with the chant. After that, foot-stamping. The floorboards, rafters and walls of the old building started to buzz and vibrate. The judges glanced at each other. Could even they control this? Would the roof fall in first?

Two more than Dennis! Two more than Dennis!

Dennis himself put a stop to it. As he mooched to the centre of the stage it was clear he was thinking hard. When he got there, he shook his head pityingly as if he knew something that made him sorry for them all. There was a clatter of chairs as kid after kid sat down again. Dennis made them wait before he spoke.

"Two marks more than me in the Prelim," he said, "but one less competitor in the Time-Trial this afternoon."

He jerked a thumb at Becca who by now was back in her place.

"I've got witnesses. Two witnesses. That so, Madboy? Weasel?"

"Sure, Dennis."

"We saw it, Dennis."

"Her bike," Dennis went on. "It'll have to be disqualified. It's remote-controlled."

"It's *what*?" said the first judge.

"Remote-controlled, mister. By one of her gang. That's definite. And the Contest is for straightforward cycles, right? So she'll have to naff off out of it."

"Are you serious, young man?"

Dennis sniffed.

"Never been more serious."

"Just wait there a moment, will you?"

The first judge beckoned to the second and they huddled at the side of the stage. Their every nod and whisper was watched. When they turned back to Dennis, there was a faint rustle along row after row as kids stiffened expectantly. The second judge pursed his lips.

"If this girl's bike were in any way remote-controlled," he said, "my examination would have revealed it. It's a . . . a strange bike, very special in a way I can't quite describe. Also it's a very handsome bike that's been beautifully looked after. But there's nothing remote-controlled about it."

"Really?" said Dennis, coolly. "Well I'll be naffed!"

"So our ruling is that there are no grounds at all for disqualifying Becca."

"You don't say," Dennis said.

"We do say. On the other hand, for making this crack-brained accusation, thereby wasting the judges' time, we consider there are grounds for disqualifying *you*."

"Oh yeah?"

"Oh yeah," said the second judge.

"Guess I'm disqualified then. As reigning champion I retire . . . *undefeated*."

Dennis's sneer seemed to fill every square centimetre of the hall.

"The crafty young tyke!" Mr Amos exclaimed. "That gets

him right off the hook. Now there will always be kids who'll think he would have been the winner if only he'd had the chance. Without Dennis, the Contest won't be the same."

"You mean all our work's been for nothing?" wailed Sharon.

"Just listen," Tim said. "The judge hasn't finished."

"Nevertheless," continued Judge Number Two, "it's occurred to us that disqualification might be just what you want."

"Eh?" growled Dennis. "Why would I want that?"

"For fear that Becca might do as well in the Time-Trial as she has in the Prelim. So despite your bad sportsmanship – which we warned you about last year, too – we will *not* disqualify you after all. However . . ." Here both judges faced the audience with a grimness that declared they were back in charge . . . "If I, or my colleague, have any repetition of the shouting and stamping and hysteria we've just seen then we'll close down the Contest immediately. Save your excitement for the Time-Trial this afternoon. We break now for lunch and meet by the Dips at two sharp. Kindly leave the hall in an orderly manner. You have been warned."

"Dennis, you and your supporters go first," added the first judge sharply. "Becca, wait till last."

It was a best-behaviour exit. As they shuffled past her, most kids gave Becca a thumbs-up sign and murmured encouragement.

"You'll get him, Becca."

"Reckon you're the new champion."

"See you at two, Becca."

"Never thought I'd see Dennis beaten."

"Fantabulous, Becca."

When the gang got outside they saw the crowd had disappeared already. No one wanted to put the Contest in danger now.

Becca stood on the hall steps and sniffed.

"Spring," she said.

But it was the Fayre she smelled too – ice-cream and hot-dogs, kebabs and candy-floss – odours that told you from now on it was open-air time for *people* not just for plants and animals. Even the clouds looked like the last of winter, huddled up for protection against the oncoming blue.

"And we're going to win," she said. "We're going to win."

"You bet we are," said Mr Amos.

"If we want to win," said Tim.

Five heads turned towards him. For Tim, he looked almost nervous.

"I've been thinking," he said. "Isn't Dennis telling the truth?"

"About what?" Sharon asked.

"About the Machine being remote-controlled. It is remote-controlled in a way, isn't it? I know it's also remote from *our* control but the point is it does have extra power. I mean, it's more than just Becca who makes it go, right? So how can it be fair for Becca to ride it in the Contest against ordinary bikes?"

"Come again?" said Georgie. "You sound like you're saying Becca *should* have been disqualified –"

"– as if she's some kind of a cheat," Leroy said.

Tim shook his head.

"Not just Becca. We're all involved."

"But wasn't it your idea in the first place to track down the Machine and tame it and then use it to beat Dennis and his Gents?" said Mr Amos.

"Yes, it was. I got carried away by the thrill of it all, I suppose. Mostly, it's my fault we're cheats. It's been bothering me for quite a while."

"So what should we do about it, son? Give up? At this stage? With every kid in the neighbourhood cheering us on

– relying on us?"

Tim nodded miserably.

"What else can we do, Mr Amos?"

"We can go ahead, that's what!" Sharon snapped. "After all the work Becca's put in and all the risks she's taken, giving up will look as if she's *chicken*! She'll get cluck-cluck-clucked everywhere she goes for the rest of her life!"

"You said it, sis," scowled Leroy. "We'll have kids flapping their arms and pecking at us day and night. Strikes me you're just jealous, Tim, 'cos it's not you who'll be riding the Machine."

"Yeah," Georgie added. "You're only saying that 'cos you don't want Becca to cop the glory. S'obvious. You're really quaint you are. First you want us to suck up to Dennis like we were blinkin' vicars or something. Now you want us to hand him the Contest on a plate."

"And who cares about your opinion, anyway?" Sharon said. "You're not our leader any more. Becca's opinion is the one that counts. It's up to her."

Suddenly they were all looking at Becca. The faces of Sharon and Georgie and Leroy were angry. Mr Amos's was angry and anxious both together. Tim's was just anxious.

Becca swallowed.

She thought of all the smiles and backslapping in the hall and what they'd change into if she withdrew from the Contest now. She thought of Tim who'd invited her into the gang last Autumn – sad, sick Tim. She thought of the others who'd made her opinion the one that counted. Also she thought of herself taking on Dennis an hour from now in front of everyone. It was up to her. Second after second piled up as she shuffled her thoughts.

Eventually, she sighed.

"Tim's right," she said. "We're cheating. But we go on with the Contest all the same. We drank to it, didn't we? To the

102

finish of Dogsmuck Doggerty? That's what matters."

At once she was surrounded by four out of five of them, being hugged and punched matily.

"Tim?" she said to the fifth. "You will be there this afternoon, won't you?"

Tim gave a weary nod.

"Sure," he said. "But I still say it's wrong. So just make sure you lick him, that's all!"

"I will," said Becca.

"You won't if you don't get some rest," said Mr Amos. "This morning took a lot out of you, I can see that. We want you fresh for two o'clock, young lady. As fresh as your Machine always is."

Becca glanced down at the Mustang Machine.

"I know where I'll rest," she said. "The perfect hideout – where no one will disturb me. Swop coats with me, Sharon: your parka for my dufflecoat. Like we did once before, remember? You can be my decoy again."

"Can't we come with you?"

"No. I want to be on my own. You lot must guard the bike. We'll meet at the Time-Trial. The place where I'm going has already brought me luck once – it's where it all started."

No one wanted to argue with the leader. As they waved goodbye and she waved back, Becca was already picturing the steep, flagstone steps and the spooky lane that led to the ruined stableyard with its one upright stall kept so tidy you'd think it was someone's den. She was sure to be safe there, wasn't she?

¶ Fourteen

At the Dips, two o'clock drew near. All round the crater of scrub and grass where the Time-Trial was based, kids jostled and chin-wagged. Above their heads pennants flapped in the breeze. Here and there were larger flags too and, spanning the starting-line and finishing-line, a pair of vast, gusty banners that proclaimed THE SECOND SPRING FAYRE CYCLE CHAMPIONSHIP.

Everyone felt good, especially Georgie and Leroy, Sharon and Mr Amos. At least they did until Dennis arrived. As soon as they saw him they knew something had gone wrong.

"He's swaggering," Sharon said.

"He's smiling," said Georgie. "That means some kid is about to be smashed."

"Or some kid has just been smashed," said Leroy.

"Where's Becca?" Tim asked.

"Yes, where's Becca?" echoed Mr Amos.

Of course, there were still five minutes to go. She could have been delayed by the crowds, they told themselves, or maybe her watch was a bit slow. Nothing to worry about yet . . . apart from Dennis's smile and his swagger. The closer he got the worse these looked.

"Well, naff me!" he declared. "Look who it isn't! Becca's fan-club complete with bike . . . but incomplete with Becca. Now where d'you reckon Becca is, Gents?"

Madboy sniggered.

"A long way from here, Dennis."

"I 'spect she's got herself all tied up," said Hogan.

"Yeah," giggled Stevie, "with a knotty problem, you might say."

"Too right," Dennis said. "My guess – an educated guess, you understand – is that she's feeling somewhat *ropy* at this instant in time. What with a *weasel* breathing down her neck an' all . . ."

"What have you done with her?" Sharon hissed.

"Who me?" said Dennis. "Just made her welcome, that's all. So welcome that now she finds it difficult to drag herself away. Mind you, I dare say she will get away in the end . . . like after the Contest is over."

"You rotten stinker!" gasped Mr Amos.

"Watch it, Grandad. Don't get your dander up too far or you'll rupture your old-age pension. Now, if you little primary school naffers will excuse me, I've got this small matter of a Time-Trial to win. And I'm bound to win now I've got a lucky charm."

From his shirt Dennis pulled a patent-leather shoe, right footed, with a scuff-mark on the toe as if it had been once used to kick something made of metal.

"On second thoughts," he went on, "you need luck a lot more than I do. In fact, you need a naffin' miracle. So you'd better have this."

Leering, he tossed-them Becca's shoe. It bounced off the handlebars of the Mustang Machine and lay in the mud.

"Proof, in case you don't believe me," Dennis said. "Like those dimbo judges didn't believe me when I told them your contraption was remote-controlled. Funny that . . . One day you'll have to tell me how it works. But not for another hour or so, okay? By then Becca may be back, you never know."

"From where?" Sharon demanded. "Where have you got her?"

"Timbuctoo," said Dennis. "Or was it Siberia? Then again it could be the Gobi Desert, I forget exactly. I'll tell you what, though. Delighted though I was when she burst in on us, all unexpected like, she's not in my den any more. She's somewhere you'll never think of looking. Cheery-bye."

Dismally, they watched him stroll towards the competitors' pen followed by his Gents and by Madboy who for some reason was carrying Dennis's bike. Already the absence of Becca was being noticed. Kids were turning their way with puzzled looks.

Then came the loudspeaker and every head swung to the starting-line. The Time-Trial had begun. For the next sixty minutes it would be skill against stopwatch for ten riders on ten bikes. Or was it only nine?

"We mustn't give up," said Sharon.

"Do we have any choice?" Leroy groaned. "What can we do, sis? It's impossible to find Becca in time even if we had a helicopter, tracker-dogs and a blinkin' house-to-house search, all operating at once."

"We've got the Machine," Sharon said.

"How can that help us?"

"By picking up Becca's trail, maybe. Give me Becca's shoe, Georgie. Ta. Now, get Becca's scent, Mustang Machine. Take a good sniff."

"A sniff?" exclaimed Georgie. "What with? First this bike's got lugholes, now it's got a conk as well. You'll be telling us next it can sing itself to sleep."

Swish-and-click, swish-and-click, swish-and-click.

"Maybe it can," said Sharon. "But right now we want it wide-awake. Tim, Mr Amos, stay here. Georgie, Leroy, come with me. And make sure one of us always keeps a grip on the Machine in case it takes off suddenly. Probably it's too late already to get Becca back before the end of the Contest but at least we can have a bash. Let's get going."

"Take care," Tim called.

"And see you soon," said Mr Amos. "We hope."

Their progress away from the Dips was strange to view. The Machine moved sometimes in spurts, sometimes doubled back on itself and sometimes stopped still as if concentrating. Was it trying to wipe out the wrong scents?

"Good job nobody else is watching them," Mr Amos said.

A roar from the crowd reminded them what everyone else was watching: the Time-Trial had claimed its first victim. A girl had overshot one of the hairpin bends, pitched over her bike's handlebars and somersaulted down the slope in a tangle of arms and legs. She wasn't injured, not seriously. Few kids ever were. What hurt was being out of the running.

After that even Tim and Mr Amos found it hard to look away. Competitor after competitor finished their practice lap then signalled for the clock to start. Their time was recorded by the judges who chalked up the fastest time so far on a board by the finishing-line. Already Dennis's record was under threat: one minute thirty seconds, only four seconds short. Two competitors later, this became one minute thirty-one point five.

"And to think Becca did it in fifty seconds dead," sighed Mr Amos. "Have they found her yet, I wonder?"

"No sign of them," Tim said.

"How long to go?"

"About a quarter of an hour, Mr Amos. Assuming there are no hold-ups."

"That's what we could do with, Tim. A whacking great hold-up. Such as those clouds over there in the west bursting on the Heath – just to delay things for a while without spoiling the Fayre altogether. Any chance do you think?"

Tim looked up. Like a huge lid edging across the sky, a cloudbank the colour of old iron was on its way from the horizon.

"Shouldn't think it'll get here fast enough."

"Pity. There goes the next competitor. Dennis's turn comes up soon."

All too soon. Another rider followed, and another. With the best lap standing at one minute thirty seconds, Dennis was summoned to the starting-line.

"So, Dennis must at least equal his own record, set last year, if he's to be the clear winner this afternoon and retain his championship," said the commentator. "But first comes his practice-run and – what's that? Just a moment everyone." The voice over the loudspeaker broke off.

"Something's up," said Mr Amos.

"Dennis was talking to the judges," Tim said. "They've sent a message to the commentary-van."

A moment later the loudspeaker crackled.

"Here are two special announcements. It seems our final competitor has not yet reported to the competitor's pen. The judges have asked me to say that she must be ready on schedule otherwise, with regret, she will be disqualified. So hurry up, young Becca – who scored full marks in the Prelim this morning, you'll remember.

"Our second announcement concerns Dennis, our reigning champion. He has indicated to the judges that he does not require a practice lap. He will compete straightaway."

"Which gives Becca even less time to get here," said Mr Amos. "What a nasty piece of work that lad is. He'll do anything to make sure Becca doesn't show him up. I could blub me eyes out."

"You'd miss some fantastic riding if you did," said Tim. "Just look at him go."

So superb was the leader of the Gents even Mr Amos couldn't resist clapping. Dennis was at top speed in an instant and took the first slope, dip and bend in the blink of an eye.

"Amazing," said Mr Amos. "Now he's going uphill faster

than some of the other kids went down – wow!"

Dennis had flung his bike into the third dip, slithered broadside-on down its slope, reversed direction round the bend at the bottom and soared over the water-jump.

"Like a bird," Mr Amos exclaimed, "but too fast for the slow section. He'll overshoot it, won't he?"

But he didn't. Pulling his bike onto its back wheel for a split-second, Dennis shimmied into and out of the figure-of-eight and slipped under the low cane across its exit as if it gaped like a goalmouth. The tree-tunnel looked as big as an underpass and the planking as broad as a motorway, so easily did he take them. When he hurled himself down the licketysplit this-way-that-way gradient of the final stretch, still one-handed, almost all the spectators knew it was the best they were ever likely to see.

"One minute ten seconds," came the announcement.

For that they'd have cheered the Devil himself. The up-roar from the Dips must have reached the village one way, and the river the other. Probably Becca herself could hear it, wherever she was.

"Poor Becca," Tim murmured.

"Poor all of us," said Mr Amos. "And that includes every-one here at the Dips."

Even the judges sensed disappointment amongst the hur-rahs. For five minutes more they put off declaring the win-ner. But eventually it had to come.

"In the absence of the final competitor, the judges award the second Spring Fayre Cycle Championship to Dennis Doggerty."

More cheers and clapping followed but now just from politeness.

"They've sussed it," Mr Amos said. "She was nobbled and they've sussed it.

"Probably," said Tim. "But perhaps it's only right that he

won."

"So he can show off and bully more than ever? If that's right then I'm a double-dutchman. I don't mind telling you that after a wait of seventy years I hoped for better than this."

The old man had his handkerchief out again. He blew his nose so hard his spectacles wobbled.

Already the crowd was beginning to leave the Dips. Most kids, as they passed, couldn't bear to utter a word though there were plenty of sympathetic grins. A few did manage to say that they knew Becca wasn't to blame.

"Try the Funfair," one suggested. "Make you feel better."

"*If* the Funfair stays open," said Mr Amos. "Look at that weather!" The cloudbank was now overhead. Half the sky was bright as Summer, the other half Winter at its darkest. And it was the dark taking over.

"I'm staying till they get here," Mr Amos said. "Even if it means a monsoon at midnight."

"It won't," said Tim. "Here they come."

Georgie wheeled the Mustang Machine, Leroy carried the rope which had tied up Becca. Their faces were glum. Becca had an arm round Sharon who shook with sobs.

"She says it's her fault," Becca explained.

"It *was* my fault. Who ordered the twins to drag the Machine away when I thought it was taking us in the wrong direction? We were battling with it for at least twenty minutes – all wasted. In the end, when we gave up, didn't it lead us straight to Becca?"

"Sure, sis, but Georgie and I thought it was a daft direction too. Who would've expected Dennis to stash Becca in Mr Amos's own backyard?"

"*My* yard?" said Mr Amos. "Jiminy cricket!"

"Exactly. Dead crafty, Dennis is. He knew we'd never think of looking there."

110

"We didn't need to think," Sharon wailed. "We needed to trust the Machine. It would have got us there and back in bags of time. But I had to interfere and foul things up, didn't I? If I hadn't been so bossy, Becca would've won the Contest."

Becca blinked back her tears.

"And if I hadn't barged smack into the Gents' hideout I wouldn't have been captured in the first place. That was the real blunder. If it's anybody's fault, it's mine. Anyway, what does it matter whose fault it was? It's all over now."

At that moment, behind them, Dennis laughed.

"All over?" he grated. "All over? Like naff it's all over. You and me have got a score to settle, darlin'. Your troubles are just beginning."

¶ Fifteen

Dennis jerked his head.

At once they were surrounded. Each of the Gents had a sneer on his lips and a mean glint in his eyes. No lip and no eye was nastier than Dennis's, though.

"Have we got shot of the judges, Madboy?" he asked.

"They just left, Dennis. Reckon we're on our own from now on."

"Good. Fetch the kids back then. All of them. Nobody must miss what I got in mind for our darlin' little Becca. Not nobody must miss that."

"No problem, Dennis. Most of them are still here, anyway."

"Madboy, I didn't say *most* of them. I said *all* of them. I have a very important message for every kid who clapped his hands and stamped his feet this morning, and our darlin' little Becca is going to help me get that message across. So just shift yourself after 'em, Madboy. If you'd be so kind."

"Sure, Dennis, sure. Hogan, Stevie – let's move!"

The round-up was hardly necessary. Already the first kids to leave the Dips had swung round, prompted by a sudden sense that this year there was to be an encore to the Contest. But now their mood was very different: once in their places, they scarcely fidgeted, scarcely spoke. Dennis's whole territory seemed to be holding its breath.

"Why don't we gang up together?" whispered Mr Amos. "Doesn't every kid here hate Dennis and his Gents?"

Becca shrugged.

"It doesn't work like that."

"I know," the old man sighed. "It never did."

Dennis especially knew it didn't work like that. His gaze shifted over the crowd as if he were counting it, person by person, to make sure it was complete. The hush was so deathly that when he smacked his lips the sound seemed to echo over the heath. No loudspeaker was needed now. Slowly, with every eye on him, he turned to Becca.

"I'm glad," he said, "that I'm not you. And when I've finished, every kid here will be glad he's not you. He will go down on his knees, put his hands together, close his eyes and thank his lucky stars he is not you. In fact, you are about to make the rest of the naffin' world very happy that they're someone else, not *you*. Get my meaning?"

"Just about," said Becca.

She tried to chuckle but her throat was too dry and it came out as a croak. Not that Dennis noticed. He was too busy working himself up.

"Yes," he went on. "In a moment or two not even you will want to be you because you are about to be smashed, bit by bit by bit – got it? In fact –"

Dennis broke off. Something Tim was doing had attracted his attention, something so strange that soon everyone was looking at Tim.

Tim was yawning.

Yawning?

Tim's voice when it came was as weary as Rip Van Winkle's.

"Oops!" he said. "Sorry Dennis. Don't let me interrupt. I know how you like to gab."

"Gab?"

"Gab, Dennis. You know – that routine of yours. The one where you try to scare kids rigid just by talking to them. You're always doing it."

"I am?"

"All the time. Right now, for example. I suppose it helps you feel like a tough guy. Don't let me stop you, though. It's quite funny, actually."

"Funny?"

"Sometimes. When it's not boring."

Dennis's eyes bulged.

"It's *boring*?" he said.

Tim nodded coolly.

"Mostly it's boring. Which is what made me yawn. But feel free to carry on – who knows, you might even end up frightening somebody!"

Dennis's mouth groped for words. Suppose Tim responded to them with another yawn, though? Or even a laugh?

Instead, Tim patted the Mustang Machine.

"Now here's something that really does scare the daylights out of me," he said. "Want to know why? Because only one person can ride it. That's Becca. According to Mr Amos any other rider would get bunged up in the air so high it would be Tuesday fortnight before they hit the ground."

"That so?" Dennis said.

"Ask Madboy and Weasel. They've seen it in action."

"It's true, Dennis," said Madboy. "It's like a bucking bronco, that bike."

"Exactly," Tim said. "Like the bucking-est bronco of them all. Now that's what I'd call real guts – someone else riding Becca's bike. Naturally, it would have to be someone who wasn't all gab . . ."

"It's a trick, Dennis!" exclaimed Madboy. "That bike's lethal. Don't fall for it!"

Tim shrugged.

"Course, it was difficult even for Becca the first time. But then she's not all gab . . . like you, Dennis."

For a split second it seemed he'd gone too far. Dennis sprang forward, hands claw-like. Then, with a giant effort, he checked himself.

"Nice one, Timothy," he hissed. "Very, very nice one. First you want to lure me into the saddle of that remote-controlled doo-hickey of yours, then you can bounce me all over the naffin' landscape. I'd have to be Dimbo of the Decade to fall for that one."

"Okay, Dennis. If you prefer to be Scaredycat of the Century, instead, that's up to you. I'll have to ride it on my own."

"On your own? You?"

"Me, Dennis. I didn't expect you take a trip on the Mustang Machine *solo*. That wouldn't be fair. I was thinking we'd ride it together, roped on for safety – one in front, one behind. That way the ride would be equally tough for both of us, wouldn't it? We'd really see which of us has got guts and which of us is all gab. What do you reckon, kids?"

"Take him on, Dennis!" someone called.

"Yeah – unless you're chicken!" called another.

Dennis swung round savagely but the remarks could have come from anywhere. He scowled. This wasn't at all what he'd planned. Could the rumours about Becca's wild super-cycle actually be true? The leader of the Gents licked his lips carefully. His eyes narrowed as he looked at Tim. That bag of bones, white as a ghost? He could out-ride him, couldn't he, so what did it matter?

"Who goes in front?" he asked.

"Me, if you like."

"Okay, then. You're on."

The crowd murmured its approval. No one quite knew what this was all about but from the look on his face Tim was up to something, and from the look on her face Becca was worried sick about it.

"Don't do it, Tim," she begged him. "You'll be pulverised!"

Tim smiled.

"Sharon was right," he said. "We've got to trust the Machine."

While Tim and Dennis settled themselves in its double saddle, Leroy, Georgie, Becca and Sharon held the Mustang Machine tight. Expertly, leaving their arms and legs free, Mr Amos tied the riders to the frame – he was used to lashing down awkward loads, he said, from his days as a totter. He hadn't had many *live* loads, though.

"Let's hope we stay that way," grinned Tim.

He winked at Becca to show he was joking. With Dennis's bulk close behind him he looked skimpier than ever. Wetness blobbed on his cheek.

"Rain," Sharon said.

"Thunder too," said Becca.

The distant rumble was like sky-size scenery shifting into place.

At first, when they let the Machine go, it didn't move.

"Gee up," snorted Dennis. "Thought you said –"

His remark was snapped off. In a scuffle of mud the Machine swung round suddenly on the spot as if it were a stallion chasing its tail. At once it twisted back, reversed, then twisted again. After this it gave a lurch, a swerve and a series of bounding hops that would have been leapfrog-like except that the Machine seemed to be bending and jumping both at the same time. Every crazy, crash-of-a-landing jarred your teeth just to see it. So how did the riders feel?

"Yippeee!" one of them called.

But which one?

Finally came up-and-over time. The Machine flipped from back-wheel to front-wheel, front-wheel to back-wheel, back-wheel to front-wheel, each bounce launching into a full somersault that turned your stomach as you watched.

"Yahooooooo!" called a rider.

At the front or the back?

Even when the Machine came to a stop no one could be sure. Tim slumped over the handlebars, his face turned away. Dennis slumped over Tim. They were trembling. Or was it the laughter of the Machine that made them shake?

"You okay?" Madboy asked his boss.

"How are you, Tim?" asked Becca.

Dennis lifted his head first. Between the blotches, his face was chalk-white. When he spoke it was through gritted teeth.

"Great. Just great. Better than anything in the Funfair. Now get me off this heap."

"So soon?" said Tim, looking up.

His skin was no pastier than usual, but then how could it be? What frightened Becca was the brightness of his eyes. Tim was back in business.

"That was just a warm-up," he said. "The proper ride's yet to come. Still fancy your chances, Dennis? Or do you want to quit now?"

Dennis swallowed.

"Course not. Let's get on with it. It's . . . it's boring hanging about."

"Oh dear," said Tim, "the last thing I want is to bore you, Dennis. Let me see . . ."

He leant back in the saddle, scanning the onlookers. His voice wasn't loud but then it didn't need to be with his audience so still, so quiet, so expectant. For suddenly even the dimmest kid there understood. The Time-Trial with its flags and cheering and stopwatches was just kid's stuff after all. This was no encore. Now, about to begin, was the real Contest.

"What about . . . the Jungle Treatment, Dennis?"

"Eh?"

"It's your favourite, isn't it? You've dished it out to plenty of people. Any kids here had the Jungle Treatment?"

At once a hand was raised. And another. Then, to right and left, more hands. In front of Tim, and behind him, hand after hand went up. He was surrounded by hands.

"Looks like a unanimous vote," said Tim. "Ever had the Jungle Treatment *yourself*, Dennis?"

"What?"

"Ever been on the receiving end?"

Tim paused to let it sink in.

"The Jungle Treatment . . ." he went on "Only special, souped up a bit – like you promised Sharon and Becca. Care of the Mustang Machine. Wave your hands, kids, if you think that would suit Dennis. Yes? Now look at that – every hand waving. Could you manage a touch of the Jungle Treatment, my beauty?"

The Machine left no doubt. It skittered friskily.

"You wouldn't dare," snarled Dennis. "*You'd be* getting the Treatment, too!"

"Just watch me. See you soon, everyone! Giddy-yap!"

"Wait!" Dennis screeched.

He was too late. Bucking, rearing and with prances to right and left, the Machine left the Dips and took off across the Heath.

By now the rain battered down, jittering across the riders' vision as they peered ahead, blinding them as they looked up. Already they felt the slow, clammy creep of it through their clothes.

"Tarzan's Waterfall," Tim called over his shoulder. "That's what we've started with. Maybe we're working through the Jungle Treatment backwards!"

Dennis didn't reply. Was he saving himself for python-the-ponk?

It wasn't long coming.

At first there seemed little to scare you – just the disused railway tunnel where Madboy had bashed up his own bike.

The Machine advanced to the bridge's centre and skipped up onto the parapet.

"Oh, no! No!" wailed Dennis.

His voice trailed away as the Machine nosedived towards the railway arch and dipped again, upside-down, into the tunnel.

They may have been out of the rain, but this was the only relief they got. Hanging with them from the roof was a dank assortment of ferns, tendrils and lumpish clusters as if the worst smells in the world had clotted there. Through these eerie, swaying stalactites the Machine picked its way. On and on it went so that goosepimple-touch after goosepimple-touch clutched at them, tightened round them, slithered over them – each bringing a whiff of the earth gone rotten. Suspended like bait, deafened by the blood rushing to their heads, they were dangled through the stench. Dennis opened his mouth to breathe, or to scream and clamped it shut again fast as something scaly slid over his tongue. This was worse than Madboy's gloves. This was worse than real snakes.

At last they reached the far arch and swung up and out into the rain and the open air.

"Spiky-spiders next," said Tim.

So where was the Machine taking them? Why, using walls and roofs as a staircase, was it mounting higher and higher up the hill?

On the topmost level of a towerblock, it let them rest awhile. From here all the city seemed spread out like a showcase for their personal inspection. What were they supposed to be looking for – tarantulas? Black widows?

Dennis shivered.

"Don't see no spiders," he said in Tim's ear.

"No," said Tim, pointing. "But I see a web."

He meant the telegraph wires, the power cables, the network of aerials that criss-crossed the roads, the streets, the highways and avenues and alleys below like the stays and halliards of sailing ships moored chock-a-block in Sharon's olden days.

"I've got it!" he said. "Waggle your hands and feet!"

"Do what?"

"Like this: my two hands and feet – plus yours. That makes eight. And that's it! *We're* the spider."

"Eh?"

"The spider is us. That's our web out there."

"You don't mean . . . all those wires and stuff?"

"I do."

Dennis was stunned.

"We're going out there? All over? Across the river even? On a bike?"

"On the Mustang Machine," said Tim.

Even as they stared, lightning forked and flickered across the greyness.

"Hey," Dennis exclaimed, "some of those lines are electrified. We could be burnt to a naffin' frazzle."

"On rubber tyres?"

"Suppose the wheel-rims make contact?"

"If they do," said Tim, "it'll be a case of *sparky*-spiders."

He didn't quite catch what Dennis said next, but there were a lot of naffs in it. Clearly, Dennis didn't much fancy the next stage in the Jungle Treatment.

"What about the elephant-walk then?" Tim asked. "Shall we transfer to that?"

As if in answer, the Machine shifted its position.

They were gazing now at the Motorway. Its surface glittered in the storm. And along it, scattering a million pinpricks of rain, came the juggernaut-lorries. They dwarfed the other traffic. From their back axles to their front bumpers, they suggested power: multi-tonnage on the move. Their gears grated. Their horns trumpeted. Stand-aside-or-else, stand-aside-or-else, stand-aside-or-else, throbbed their engines.

"Those are the elephants?" breathed Dennis.

"You bet," Tim grinned. "Can't you see it, Dennis? Nipping in and out amongst them? Maybe, with the Machine keeled over, we could even slip *beneath* them. Imagine that!"

Dennis could imagine it. He saw complex suspension just above his head and on either side of him huge, shoulder-high tyres rolling past . . . just missing. Or not.

"Which first, then?" asked Tim. "Spiky-spiders or the elephant-walk?"

Frazzled or flattened? To Dennis it seemed a naff of a choice.

"Bikes on telegraph wires?" he said desperately. "Or on motorways? It's against the law."

Tim shrugged.

"So's what you do – Dennis and his Gents. Bullying kids is against the law."

"Yeah, but we don't kill people."

"Who says the Machine will kill us? It's not an ordinary bike, remember. Of course, it might frighten us a bit. There's plenty to be frightened of."

In his soft, matter-of-fact voice Tim predicted exactly what would frighten them. How could he know such details . . . had he done this before? Soon the thunder of the juggernauts filled Dennis's ears and high-wire lightning flashed before his eyes. This was the gab of all gabs.

When he'd finished, Tim twisted round.

"Ready then?" he asked.

Dennis said nothing. "Mind you," said Tim, "we could always stop now."

"Now?"

"Sure Dennis. Go back to the others. We'll call it quits

121

a draw."

"Me . . . and you? A draw?"

"That's right. Shake on it?"

For a moment it was touch and go with Dennis as he swayed in the saddle. Then, mustering all the strength he had left, he straightened up. The hand he offered wasn't for shaking. It was a fist with two fingers for a claw.

"Get naffed," he whispered.

Tim shook his head sadly.

"Dennis," he said. "You're forcing me to win it *your* way. Isn't *my* way better for both us? Please, Dennis. You won the Contest . . . make this a draw can't you? Honours even?"

"Go naff yourself"

"Okay," sighed Tim. "If that's what you want."

A light tap from his heels was enough to stir the Mustang Machine.

Swish.

Click.

Swish-and-click.

Swish-and-click, swish-and-click, swish-and-click . . .

Plus screaming.

Two voices *screaming* . . . on and on.

Not just for spiky-spiders and the elephant-walk, but eventually all the way back to the Dips, where, drenched with rain, everyone still waited. Not a kid had moved.

"What's happened to Tim and Dennis?" Becca exclaimed.

Whatever it was, it had left their eyes shut tight, their jaws clenched with shock.

"Leave the ropes to me," said Mr Amos. "I've untied knots all my life."

Even so, it was several minutes before they were free. At once Dennis slid from the bike, sprawling headlong. Tim seemed frozen where he was.

"How was it, Dennis?" asked Madboy. "Good ride?"

"You naffer," Dennis groaned.

"Sorry, Dennis," said Madboy hastily. "Just thought I'd ask. Give me a hand, Weasel. Help me get him on his feet."

"Not on his feet," said Tim. "Get him back on the bike."

"What?"

"On the bike. It's not over yet."

Nothing shifted except the rain. All over the Dips, kids stood shoulder to shoulder, but only Tim and Dennis seemed to exist.

"That was our *practice lap*, Dennis," continued Tim. "Now comes the *real* Trial: a lap without the rope."

"Without the . . ."

Dennis jerked himself up onto his elbows and stared, wild-eyed.

"Without the rope?" he gasped. "On that thing? You're mad!"

"Me?" said Tim. "Not me, Dennis. I wanted to settle for a draw, remember? You were the one who refused. So now we've got to find the winner, right? And shouldn't the next lap do it? Or the next but one, maybe, when we ride one-handed? Or no hands at all after that? One of us is sure to give up eventually. So get on the bike, Dennis."

"You're bluffin', that's what you're up to! Bluffin'!"

Tim shook his head. Under the plastered-down hair, his eyes were so blank, his cheeks so pale and his lips so tight with strain, his face looked like a skull under a wig.

"Try me," he said.

Slowly, Dennis got to his feet. He managed one step, two steps forward. His hands, as he stretched it towards the Machine, twitched.

"You've . . . you've got to be bluffin'," he said hoarsely.

"Get on the bike, Dennis."

As Dennis lifted his leg across the saddle, he flinched suddenly as if he smelled lightning again or caught the stink of heavy, loadbearing rubber. Without a safety-rope this time ... ?

"No," he whimpered. "No."

He staggered back, his hands over his face.

"Get on the bike, Dennis," said Tim. "Or tell them I've won."

From behind the hands came a muffled sob.

"Tell them, Dennis!"

Another sob.

"Tell them!"

"You've won!" Dennis screamed. "You naffin' naff of a naffer! You've won!"

There was no burst of applause, no uproar – just a long, long sigh as if everyone could relax now. Dennis turned, still hiding his face, and plunged down the slope towards the Heath. Not till his lurching, stumbling figure was out of sight did anyone move.

Madboy sniffed.

"He's forgotten his bike," he said. "He'll have to come back for it, won't he."

With that for their goodbye, the Gents left.

Only then did the crowd wake up: kids laughed, kids slapped each other on the back, kids yelled hip-hip-hooray to Tim. Some joined in singing with Sharon:

"Dennis Dogsmuck, Boo Hoo!
Dennis Dogsmuck – you're through!
When it came to the proper Contest
Tim was better than you!"

Lying back on the parkas and dufflecoats and anoraks they'd spread out for him, Tim smiled wrily.

"I'm not," he said. "In a way I came out on top because I was *worse* than Dennis – also because I had nothing to lose, really."

124

"Save your breath," said Mr Amos. "The ambulance will soon be here."

While they were waiting for it, Tim did his best to keep them amused. He'd have gone back to the hospital soon anyway, he said, so why get upset about it? To cheer them up, he told them funny stories – especially about the last amazing ride of the Mustang Machine. But always the jokes were about his terror, never Dennis's. He made them laugh so much they were still chuckling when the ambulance pulled away.

"Bye, Tim!" they shouted.

"Bye, Tim!" echoed the Dips.

"See you, Tim!"

"See you!"

"Hey," Sharon said, "what's happened to the Machine?"

"Gone," said Mr Amos. "Didn't you see Tim wave farewell to it? Look, you can just catch a glimpse of it if you're quick."

He pointed to a dot on the horizon no bigger than a pin-prick. Was that the Mustang Machine?

"Hey!" exclaimed Georgie. "What about the herd of Mustang Machines down by the river. Did Tim really see one bike for each of us, d'you reckon?"

"Do leave off," said Leroy. "He just said that to make us feel good."

"I . . . don't know," Becca said.

The wail of the ambulance had faded now, but if she screwed up her eyes she could still make out its blue light flashing fuzzily in the rain.

"Anything's possible," she grinned. "Sure as brake-blocks are brake-blocks, anything's possible."

All About Barn Owl Books

If you've ever scoured the bookshops for that book you loved as a child
or the one your children wanted to hear again and again and been
frustrated then you'll know why Barn Owl Books exists. We are hoping
to bring back many of the excellent books that have slipped from
publishers' backlists in the last few years.

Barn Owl is devoted entirely to reprinting worthwhile out-of-print
children's books. Initially we will not be doing any picture books,
purely because of the high costs involved, but any other kind of children's
book will be considered. We are always on the lookout for new titles and
hope that the public will help by letting us know what their own special
favourites are. If anyone would like to photocopy and fill in the form
below and give us their suggestions for future titles we would be delighted.

We do hope that you enjoyed this book and will read our other
Barn Owl titles.

Books I would like to see back in print include:

_____

_____

_____

Signature

_____

Address

_____

_____

Please return to Ann Jungman, Barn Owl Books
15 New Cavendish Street, London W1M 7AL

Barn Owl Books

THE PUBLISHING HOUSE DEVOTED ENTIRELY TO
THE REPRINTING OF CHILDREN'S BOOKS

RECENT TITLES

The Spiral Stair – Joan Aiken
Giraffe thieves are about! Arabel and her raven have to act fast

Your Guess is as Good as Mine – Bernard Ashley
Nicky gets into a stranger's car by mistake

Voyage – Adèle Geras
Story of four young Russians sailing to the US in 1904

Private – Keep Out! – Gwen Grant
Diary of the youngest of six in the 1940s

Leila's Magical Monster Party – Ann Jungman
Leila invites all the worst baddies to her party and they come!

You're thinking about doughnuts – Michael Rosen
Frank is left alone in a scary museum at night

Jimmy Jelly – Jacqueline Wilson
A T.V. personality is confronted by his greatest fan